CRAVED

CRAVED

ADAM & ELLA FOUR

Emily Jane Trent

Camden Lee Press, LLC
12112 N. Rancho Vistoso Plaza Ste. 150-101
Oro Valley, AZ
www.EmilyJaneTrent.com

Publisher's Note: This is a work of fiction. Names, characters, places, and incidents are a product of the author's imagination. Locales and public names are sometimes used for atmospheric purposes. Any resemblance to actual people, living or dead, or to businesses, companies, events, institutions, or locales is completely coincidental.

Craved/Emily Jane Trent. -- 1st ed.

ISBN-13: 978-1496080325

ISBN-10: 1496080327

To Hot Chapter, my awesome street team.

ACKNOWLEDGMENTS

No book is published in isolation. So many helped me, some in ways they never imagined. From my friends and family, my mentor, and a long list of indie authors, all have contributed to my success. Without my editor, cover artist, formatting expert, and others who played a part in making this book, I'd never be able to create these books for you like I do. I want to thank each of them for their good work.

I want to take a moment to let my readers how much I appreciate them. You – all of you – are awesome! Every day I read emails and posts from you telling me how much you enjoy my books. It means everything. And it's amazing motivation. If I am using a lot of enthusiastic words here, it is because of the feeling I have for you. Sharing these stories, and knowing you love them and want more, chokes me up (yes, with real tears) - I'm moved. Thank you!

I am yours, Adam...I'll always be yours. -Ella

Chapter 1

Adam stood on the deck by the pool, gazing out at the glassy bay glimmering under the expansive blue sky. The weather was as warm as expected for April in Rio, but late in the day there would likely be showers. Though she'd only been gone for a couple of hours, he missed Ella.

Sitting on the flat pool edge, Adam reflected on the joy he'd experienced since proposing to her on the deck of his yacht in Newport, months before. The truth was he craved Ella, with every part of his body and soul. And he never dreamed he'd be lucky enough to spend his life with her.

With the wedding only a week away, Adam looked forward to being married to the woman he was so in love with. Maybe he should be nervous, but only excitement rattled his otherwise peaceful state. After a long battle, with Ella by his side, they'd rid their life of Claudio, his evil-hearted father. Since then, and for the first time in Adam's life, he had been able to live unencumbered by oppression.

Ella was the reason he had fought so hard. Whatever darkness haunted his youth, Adam would not allow it to shadow his love. When his father's demands threatened the woman he cared about more than anything, and his dear family as well, something had to be done. Together,

Adam and Ella had achieved their goal and pushed Claudio into an untenable position. He'd fled to Paraguay and had no hope of returning.

Thus, Adam felt as secure as he ever could in the unsettled city of Rio. Brazil was his home, and Ella had come to love the country and the people as much as he did. Vibrant with life, the culture was warm and friendly. Any excuse for a party or celebration was seized upon, and since they'd been back, Adam and Ella had partied to their fill.

It had taken months to prepare for the wedding, and still there were last-minute items to attend to. Fiorella was shopping with Ella, taking care of a few things that could not be delegated. Plus, she would have fun. Adam thought of how happy Ella had been since agreeing to marry him, and his heart swelled. It wouldn't be long and they'd seal the union with all their family and friends there to witness. Every man should be so fortunate.

Most of the morning, Adam had worked in his office, making progress on some new software, plus debugging some recently implemented banking programs. He stood and stretched, taking one more look across Guanabara Bay, having a clear view of the mountains and the city. The view was unparalleled and he never tired of it.

He strolled and grabbed a cold coconut drink from the refrigerator to quench his thirst in the warm weather. His chef had been stocking up on them, knowing they were a favorite of Ella's. And Adam grew to enjoy them as well. It shouldn't be long before Ella returned, and maybe they'd go down to the beach. He had a stack of mail on the desk, so he sat in his chair and rifled through his drawer for the letter opener.

Adam took a big gulp of the refreshing drink and put it on the glass desktop. Leaning back in his chair, he began opening the first item. Nothing much, just a confirmation that he'd asked Quinn to forward to him. A few items were the usual junk. All the bills went directly to his accountant so he didn't have to deal with them.

One envelope had a local postmark, but no return address. Adam's name and mailing address were typed, so it was possibly business related. Most such correspondence was conducted via his attorney's office, and Quinn would notify him of anything requiring his attention. Interested, Adam sliced it along the top side and slid out a one-page letter.

Puzzled, he unfolded it. The message, written in Portuguese, was not typed or handwritten; it was composed of cutout letters from a Brazilian magazine. Instantly, Adam thought of spy movies where the criminals disguise who they are by using that method of communication. As he read through, deciphering the words made from the colorful letters of various sizes, cut inexpertly from the shiny pages of various publications, the message began to form.

Unmoving, Adam read it again. And again. No, it couldn't be. His pulse pounded and his heart fell, the peace he'd known instantly shattered by several ill-constructed sentences. The tone was threatening and held added horror in the jagged, oddly arranged paper letters. The demand was clear: *You will pay.*

Panic raged in Adam's chest, followed by anger. The knowledge that his father dared to invade their life, yet again, was intolerable. There was too much to lose. It wasn't about money; it was about those Adam loved, Ella most prominently. And he had no intention of tolerating his father's bullying.

The letter in his hands, written by Claudio, raised a question. Since the letter had a local postmark, did that mean his father had returned to Rio? Or did it mean he had someone working with him, someone who could cross the border and deliver the untimely threats? Adam guessed it was the latter.

Stunned, Adam didn't do anything at first. His mind raced, and his first thought was of Ella. For the moment, she was likely safe. Nico and two others from the team were guarding the women during the shopping outing. In

Rio, there was always danger; it was that kind of city. Yet his security didn't know there was any unusual risk.

The first action Adam would take would be to contact Nico to alert him and require that he bring the women home. But request that he not tell Ella the reason. That was something Adam preferred to do personally. Still Adam hesitated, having trouble making sense of what was happening. His father had been chased to Paraguay, burdened with gambling debts and broke.

That he had managed to survive the wrath of strong men, also part of the criminal underworld, was amazing enough. But it seemed he had a new ally, at least one, that was willing to perpetrate the evil deed of threatening Adam and his family, plus seeing the threat through, if it came to that. At a minimum, the accomplice had mailed the bizarrely created letter from Rio.

The worst was the stated intent if Adam did not pay: *You will never see Ella again.* The ugly words blotted out the beauty of his life with Ella, and sucked the peace away with it. Increasing the torment was the fact that the letter did not state the amount of the demand, only that Adam would be contacted again with specific instructions.

Somehow, he needed to tell her about the threat without overly frightening her. And that would be difficult. Ella was smart and wouldn't easily be deluded into thinking everything was all right. Nothing was right, now that Claudio had pierced the joy that surrounded them, and cast gloom over Adam's life once again.

Only seconds passed, seeming like protracted minutes, when Adam picked up his phone to call Nico. There was one thing Adam knew for sure—he would not allow his father to harm Ella. Or any member of his family, for that matter. This was a fight Claudio could not win. Adam had too much at stake.

Chapter 2

Nine months earlier...

Late summer temperatures in Newport were warm. It was the best time of year to be at the beach. Each morning after sunrise, Ella grabbed her board and raced Adam to the shore. Surfing hadn't lost its charm, nor had Adam. It had only been days since he'd asked her to be his wife, and the exhilaration of being in love consumed her.

The waves were subdued, but Ella didn't care. She was with Adam, which was the only thing that really mattered. Swells would be better once fall came, and even bigger in the winter. There was so much to look forward to. Every day was special, even more so since they could enjoy each other without fear. The constant threat they'd been under since the day they'd met had been a drag on the joy that filled their hearts.

But no more. Claudio was banished to Paraguay, out of their life. For so long, Adam's father had been a source of gloom. Now it was over. And Ella couldn't wait to tell her friend the news of her engagement. She could have called, but preferred to see Kaiyla's face when she flashed her ring. As she cruised toward the coffee shop in the red

Ferrari, the diamond sparkled in the sun, making Ella smile.

Kaiyla had to work later but had an hour free—just enough time. After parking in the far corner of the lot, cautious of not being near other cars and getting the door dinged, Ella hopped out and clicked the locks. Swinging her purse over her shoulder, she jogged across to the shop. When she opened the door, she spotted Kaiyla in line and sneaked up to surprise her.

"Hey, Ella," her friend said with a giggle. "I didn't see you."

"Just got here."

Ella noticed her friend's hairdo; her blond hair was kind of long and spiky. Working in a salon, Kaiyla was continually trying new looks. Or maybe it was that she liked to try different styles all the time, thus she was a perfect fit for her job as a hairdresser.

"Love the hair."

Kaiyla brushed back the long bangs. "Do you? I'm not sure yet. The long bangs are in style, but it's hard to see." She giggled again, her green eyes sparkling.

With the drinks ordered, they moved down the counter to pick them up, then spotted a table by the window. Both slid into wooden chairs and draped their purses over the backs. Ella could wait no longer.

She held her left hand out and grinned.

Kaiyla shrieked and lifted her friend's hand for a closer look. "Oh my God, you're kidding me! Adam?"

Ella nodded. "Yes."

"When?"

"Just a couple days ago. Friday, when we went out on the yacht."

"How romantic."

"It was. You can't believe it. He put the ring in a dessert dish with a covered dome. And when I lifted the lid, there it was."

"Wow. Adam."

"I still can hardly believe it."

"When's the wedding?"

"Not sure yet. Adam has a lot going on, business stuff. We haven't set a date yet. He told me in Brazil that couples are usually engaged *for years* before they get married."

Kaiyla's joyful expression disappeared. "Years?"

Ella continued to smile.

"But you aren't Brazilian."

"No, I'm not. And he told me we don't have to wait that long."

Kaiyla's smile returned. "Whew, you scared me."

"What about you and Steve?"

"Oh, like I've said, he is doing his medical internship. That takes a lot of focus. But once he gets through that, then we are definitely getting married." Kaiyla took a sip of her iced drink. "The only thing is I'll have to be patient. The internship takes a long time. You'll probably be married before me."

"Probably." Ella swigged from her cup.

"Anxious, are we?"

Ella laughed. "Yes and no. It's a big step. I have no doubts about Adam. It's going to be amazing being his wife. But being engaged is fun, too."

"I'm so proud of you."

Ella raised her eyebrows.

Kaiyla put her cup on the table and leaned forward. "I mean that in a good way. You know you've overcome a lot. And you deserve all the happiness life can offer. Adam is one of the best things that ever happened to you."

"I am lucky. Really, you know me. I never dreamed I'd meet a man like Adam, much less marry him. And I had to fight for it."

"You mean his father?"

"Exactly. We haven't had it easy, at least in the beginning. But it's going to be wonderful from now on."

"I know it will." Kaiyla took several sips. "And a bit of other news, Cameron and Lori seem really good together. I can see it even more since they moved in together. I get the feeling he might pop the question before too long."

"He's a good guy. Glad he found someone right for him. He's managing the bookstore still, right?"

"Yeah. And the way he tells it, the place has a whole new life. I think Zoe was getting tired of it, wanted to move on. But Cameron gets a kick out of it. The coffee shop they added on is doing well, and it's a good source of income."

"What about his photography?"

"He still does that too. Maybe it will turn into something full time later, but now he does it in off hours. I've seen some of his recent stuff. It's pretty good."

"Do you know if he got those pictures I sent him of Botafogo Bay?"

Kaiyla nodded with a mouthful of liquid. "Mmm. Yep. Really liked them. That's so cool how you send him photos from all these places in Brazil."

"Lots to take pictures of there. I thought he'd like them." Ella leaned back, with her left palm on the table so she could admire her ring. Just seeing it on her finger made her happy. "What about Zoe? Heard anything from her?"

"She's sent some postcards to Cameron, and I think they've talked or emailed. If he has any questions about the business, he can go to her. But I think he's pretty much got the hang of it. The last card she sent was from Paris."

"I knew she wanted to travel. I'm glad she's getting a chance to do that."

"Well, I can't get over your news. Congratulations!" Kaiyla beamed.

"I wanted to tell you in person."

"I'm glad you did." The two chatted about other things to catch up, then remembering where she had to be, Kaiyla grabbed her purse. "Well, gotta run. I have a client at Beach Beauty. Maybe when Steve gets through his internship I won't have to do this anymore. I could be a lady of leisure."

"Definitely." Ella stood and hugged her friend. "Call me soon. Maybe we can all go out. You can invite Cameron and Lori, too."

Kaiyla nodded and started for the door. "We'll do that some night...love you," she called back.

"Love you, too." Ella delighted in how Kaiyla's accent surfaced now and then. She hadn't been to Texas in years, yet the influence was still there. When she said the word "night" it sounded like "naht." She watched Kaiyla disappear around the corner, then dumped the rest of her drink and crossed the lot to her car.

*****

A couple of weeks later, Ella visited her mother, and was glad to see she seemed to be doing okay. It was a first for her not to be living with a man. But for the time being, Jeanne seemed satisfied staying with her friend Margie, who was also single. Taking her mother to lunch was new for Ella.

While growing up, Ella had never experienced the usual mother/daughter things. Her mother's love life had always come first. Now it seemed there was time for her daughter, and it was kind of nice. So far the investment money from her father's estate seemed to be sufficient support, but Ella reassured her mother that she would help if needed.

After all, she was a published author now, and her book was doing quite well. Ella was considering a sequel, but was putting it off until after the wedding. Jeanne seemed pleased over the news of Adam's proposal. And she hoped to attend the wedding. There wasn't much more Ella could hope for. Just the fact that she was developing a relationship with her mother, so late in life, was enough.

Following that successful encounter, Ella asked Adam to drive her to San Diego to see Julianna. Her sister was all grown up now, and truly beautiful. Her flawless skin and blue eyes, along with honey-blond hair, made Ella remember why she'd been jealous of her when they were younger. Yet things had changed. Having Adam meant so much, and wrapped in his love, Ella felt beautiful too—for the first time in her life.

She no longer had reason to be jealous, and only wanted to be a real sister to Julianna. Being with Adam and his family in Rio, and witnessing the affection they felt for each other, had encouraged Ella to make a better effort with her sister. And it had paid off.

Julianna had matured as well, and no longer harbored resentment. In fact, when Adam took a walk, leaving them alone to talk, her sister brought up the subject. They both knew when Ella had left home, it had caused bad feelings.

"I know you feel I abandoned you," Ella said. "And, in a way, I guess I did."

"I don't blame you. Not anymore. It was hard then. Dad was impossible to live with, and, well, you know what mother was like in those days."

Ella nodded.

"But that was so long ago. If I had been the older one, I'm sure I would have left, too. I mean, come on, who would have stayed in that household if they didn't have to?" Julianna hugged her sister, the most affection she'd shown since the day Ella had moved out.

"Thank you for understanding." Ella leaned back. "And you're coming to the wedding, right?"

"Of course. When is it?"

Ella laughed. "I'm not sure yet. But we will let you know."

"Where is it?"

"I don't know that either. We are still deciding. But I will give you plenty of notice."

"Okay, then. I'm so glad you came to see me, and that I got a chance to meet Adam. He seems very nice, and I can tell he adores you."

"I hope so." Ella squeezed her sister's hand. "Because I'm crazy about him."

*****

The lazy days in Newport were filled with swimming, surfing, and soaking up the sun on the beach. Somehow Adam managed to get in plenty of work time, creating new software, securing new deals, and coordinating with his sales team, as needed. When he was secluded in his home office, Ella took the chance to work on the promotion of *Dare To Love*, her romance novel. It still surprised her that it sold as well as it did.

But it shouldn't have. The romance she poured into the story had surged from her own heart, brought to life by her true-life love story with Adam. It was clear to her that she had written emotion she understood, and her readers felt it. Later there would be more novels, but first she planned to spend time promoting the current one.

Although Adam's chef cooked for them, on some nights Ella took over. While in Brazil, Adam's sister had taught her how to cook, and she could create dishes in several different cuisines, including Brazilian, Italian, and American. She'd learned how to make some of the tastiest Portuguese-influenced seafood dishes. Grilled codfish in a mayonnaise sauce wasn't too difficult, and could always be counted on to be tasty.

It was a different lifestyle for Ella, though. She'd known Adam was wealthy, but he never acted like it. He was so down to earth, and if she hadn't known he had so much money, she'd never have guessed. Without a shred of arrogance, wearing board shorts with cotton shirts most of the time, he hardly looked like he was rich.

But he did keep a staff, so Ella had to get used to not having to clean or even wash clothes. Everything was done, and Adam had even hired security to keep them safe. After all that had happened in Brazil, he wasn't taking any chances. Even when Ella drove to see Kaiyla, or went shopping, she was allowed to drive the car, but security followed. It was like being a celebrity, only she wasn't famous.

Despite all of that, nothing got in the way of their desire for each other. There was no rush to get married, as they were thoroughly enjoying their engagement. Ella's love for Adam grew, if that were possible. She loved him completely, yet found that each moment, each day, she loved him more. It was magical. And the best part was that Adam felt the same, and demonstrated his love in many ways.

The season changed to fall, and though surfing was still a daily ritual, both of them wore wetsuits in the cold ocean water. One morning after hitting the waves, they changed into warm clothes, and Ella scrambled eggs to share breakfast with Adam. After swigging orange juice, she said, "Guess what?"

Adam shoveled in a big mouthful of eggs. He shrugged.

"She emailed back."

"Who did?"

"Natalie." Not long before, Adam had secured a software contract with Tanner of Clarke Luxury Brands as a result of Ella's encouragement. His wife, Natalie Baker, was one of her favorite dress designers, and that was reason enough in Ella's mind for Adam to agree to do business with Tanner.

"Oh." Adam took a big gulp of juice. "What did she say?"

"She will do it. Can you believe it? *The* Natalie Baker is going to design *my* wedding dress." Ella jumped up from her chair and gave Adam a big hug, as if he were responsible for the good news.

"That is great." Adam frowned. "How will that work? Do you have to go see her?"

Ella realized in that moment that if such were required, Adam would make it happen. It seemed there was no end to what he would do to make her happy. She knew she had a silly grin on her face, but she couldn't help it.

"No, I don't have to go there. She says I need to get a seamstress to take my exact measurements. Then send as much detail as possible about what I want. Based on all that, she will create a design for me."

"I know it will be beautiful." Adam grinned and pulled

Ella close to kiss her. "But then, anything on you would be beautiful."

"Well, I couldn't be more pleased. It's going to be the perfect dress. Once I get the design details I can have the dress made and fitted in time for the wedding." Ella cocked her head to one side. "When are we getting married, anyway?"

"Hmm, good question. I am rather enjoying the engagement."

Ella kissed him tenderly, knowing it would lead to more.

"Me too," she whispered.

Chapter 3

Adam didn't need a special reason to take Ella out to one of the many fine restaurants in Newport Beach; being in love was enough. Thus, they frequented many of the establishments, enjoying everything from pizza and burgers to gourmet cuisine. Reservations at Bay Bistro one night meant Ella could wear one of her new dresses.

There was a time when her wardrobe consisted of shorts and shirts, but after meeting Adam that had gradually changed. At first it felt odd to wear nicer attire. After all, Ella had never considered she was beautiful. Whether her opinion had changed or not, it was clear that Adam saw beauty when he looked at her, and she wished to encourage him.

On numerous occasions, Ella had gone shopping with Kaiyla, since she needed her advice on what looked good and what didn't. Her friend was more comfortable with fashion and had talent with hair, makeup, and clothes. Wanting to look her best, Ella welcomed guidance, and it was given.

Newport Beach had no shortage of places to shop, having everything from luxury retail shopping malls to bargain stores. Low-cost choices had been Ella's prior experience. But being with Adam demanded something better. It pleased him to see her in nice clothes, and his admiration when she wore them was all the motivation she needed.

The options were endless, and she'd even been to Fashion Island, a premier outdoor coastal shopping destination with a blend of specialty boutiques. Kaiyla had been tireless, and they came home loaded with purchases. Ella's closet was starting to fill up.

A couple of times Adam even took her out, though his idea of shopping bore little resemblance to Kaiyla's. He guided her through some high-end shops in Corona del Mar and waited outside the dressing rooms for her to model each item. Ella had never had a man want to buy her clothes, but Adam did, and he gave his credit card to the clerks with a smile.

*****

For dinner at the bistro, Ella wore one of the dresses Adam had particularly liked. It was an emerald-green dress by Anne Klein made from stretchy material. The sleeves covered her upper arms, and the hem stopped just above the knee with slits on each side.

What made it sensual was that the fabric clung to her body, caressing every curve. Really, it gave her curves she didn't even have. It did look good with her brown hair and softly tanned skin; even she thought so. With gold heels, it was perfect for a night out.

Ella let her hair flow free the way Adam liked it, and she wore makeup how Kaiyla had showed her. She was really looking forward to the evening. Even more so when she saw Adam. After taking a step from the bathroom where she made a last check on how she looked, Ella stopped.

The beige chinos Adam wore stretched over his thighs, and the tight fabric drew her attention to his masculine shape. Paired with an ivory fitted tee made of shiny material, and a sand-colored blazer, the look was casually dressy. And very sexy. The blazer was draped over his broad shoulders and full biceps, accenting his leanly muscled shape.

The look in his eyes matched the mood his attire conveyed: lustful. Which was precisely how Ella felt.

"You look..." Ella stopped, mouth open, unable to come up with a description that fit the image of masculinity standing before her.

A bare hint of a smile turned the corners of his mouth, and his amber eyes gleamed. Adam took a step closer, and Ella's heart pounded.

"Amore mia," he said. "You look amazing."

The kiss he gave her nearly made her forget they were on the way to dinner.

"Ready?" Adam asked, leaving her gasping from the touch of his warm lips, but not releasing her.

Ella nodded, never taking her eyes from his.

*****

Their reservations were early, so they were seated in time for sunset. The table was next to huge windows with a view of the bay, and they enjoyed watching the sky dim as the bright yellow sun lowered. The blue above turned lavender, and the horizon blazed with yellow and orange before the sun dipped below the horizon.

Adam squeezed her hand, and Ella sighed.

"It's just too romantic." She gazed around at the candlelit room and the tables covered with white linen decorated with small vases of flowers.

Adam lifted her hand and kissed her knuckles. "I love you so much."

Gazing into his soft eyes, his golden hair lightly messy and so touchable, Ella felt weak. "I love you, too."

The waitress interrupted the intimate moment by arriving with the French Sauvignon Blanc they'd ordered. She proceeded with the ritual of opening it with a fancy cork puller and allowing Adam to have the first taste, then pouring some for each of them. As she walked away, Adam sniffed the cork and offered it to Ella.

It was an experience, that was for sure. Swirling her wine, Ella picked up an aroma that reminded her of herbs. The first sip was refreshing, but she couldn't place the taste.

"Grassy?" Adam asked, holding up his glass to examine the wine's color.

Ella nodded. "Yes, I think so. I wouldn't have thought of that, but now that you said it, I recognize it."

They continued to sip wine and enjoy each other's company. On some occasions they had been known to talk endlessly. But for some reason, that evening it was enough just to be together.

The mushroom-crusted wild Chilean sea bass was served in a timely fashion, and it came with perfectly cooked asparagus and flavored mashed potatoes that the menu referred to as *potato puree*. Each bite was delicious, but tasted even more exquisite because Ella felt slightly giddy in the light of Adam's love. Plus, the wine gave her a bit of a buzz, upping her enjoyment.

But even the lovely atmosphere, gourmet food, and fine wine couldn't distract her from Adam. He was, without a doubt, a heartthrob. Sun and surf agreed with him, and his skin was lightly bronzed. His amber eyes and pale hair combined to make him impossibly handsome. Ella couldn't wait to get him home.

The evening drifted by, and in a leisurely fashion they finished the meal and sipped espressos, passing on dessert. After paying, Adam escorted her to the lobby. Since they'd been spending so much time at the beach house, he'd purchased a silver Audi A8 with gray leather seats. The security guard, who had driven, pulled along the curb and opened the door for them.

In Rio there had been even more of a need for security, and with reliable staff covering hours on a regular basis, Ella had become friends with some of them. In Newport, it was different. Adam used a reputable company, and guards worked shifts in rotation. Though Ella began to recognize some of them, she didn't know them by name.

They did their job in a fairly unobtrusive manner.

The fall season brought cooler weather, but it was warm in the back of the Audi. And Ella's need for Adam had her heated up anyway. She held his hand on the short ride home, feeling his warmth and knowing his desire equaled hers. When the driver pulled into the enormous garage facility and rolled into one of the many empty parking spaces, Adam risked looking over at Ella.

The lust in his gaze melted her, making her hesitate for a moment when the driver opened her door. Averting her eyes from Adam's piercing look, she slid out and waited for him to follow. Giving a nod to the guard, he put his arm around her to guide her inside. Ella's heart pounded.

Once in the main room, Ella slipped off her shoes and watched Adam take his off, too, and remove his blazer. The fitted shirt wrapped over his chest and his stiff nipples poked into the fabric. It was difficult to resist just ripping his clothes off, but she also enjoyed the process. With Adam it was always special.

He led her to the dining room, which piqued her curiosity. His eyes gleaming with desire, Adam pulled out one of the padded chairs and Ella cooperated by sitting down. He stood before her, and the bulge in his slacks was eye level. The urge to reach out and squeeze him was powerful, but something held her back.

Under the intensity of his gaze, Ella sat riveted, waiting to follow his lead. The beach house was silent except for the crash of the waves outside, which could be heard through the open glass door. Spellbound, she drank in the sight of the gorgeous man standing over her. When he reached out and ran his fingertips along her jaw, Ella closed her eyes.

The scent of him was intoxicating, an erotic combination of musky cologne and maleness. Her fingers itched to touch him, yet holding back was highly arousing. Ella felt his soft mouth touch hers, and she parted her lips, welcoming him. His kiss was burning hot, and their tongues raked together in a soulful plea for more.

Adam placed his palms against her cheeks and got down on his knees. She leaned over to kiss him again, searching and delving into his mouth. He tasted so good, slightly of alcohol, more of male. She dug her hands into his hair, no longer able to resist touching, and he moaned, rewarding her.

Plunging his hands into her long hair, Adam pulled her back and proceeded to ravage her neck with kisses. An electric pulse surged through her body and pounded between her legs. Still fully clothed, she wished he would palm her breasts and press over her taut nipples. As if knowing her thought, Adam drifted lower and bit her nipples through the stretchy material of her dress.

Ella whimpered and arched her back. "Adam."

The feel of his tongue along the inner side of her forearm was a surprise, and warmth spread through her lower body. Adam licked up and down her tender skin then switched to the other forearm. Just his tongue raking along her arm drove her crazy.

"Adam."

Slowing, he swirled his tongue around the inside of her wrist, first one and then the other. Such was her arousal that Ella was desperate for him to do more. If only he would take her clothes off, or even just reach under her dress and touch her. Anything. But his teasing ministrations were intolerable. Yet he continued. He sucked at the tips of her fingers, one by one, as if he had all the time in the world.

Ella gasped for some relief, but he gave her none. When he had pushed her to the edge of endurance, Adam ran his fingers down her calves and ankles. Then back up. She shuddered with pleasure at such a simple gesture. Needing more, wanting everything, Ella tipped her head back.

Adam rose on his knees and licked over her collarbone. Running her hands over his body, she felt his firm muscle, and her clit tightened. She thought she'd die if he didn't do more soon. But, mercilessly, he kissed the sensitive skin of her neck and stopped intermittently to nibble. If he had bitten her, it would not have been too much.

At that moment, she wanted Adam to consume her, and she was prepared to give all. He caressed the curve of her ear and tugged one earlobe with his teeth. Her panting sped up, and her muscles turned to jelly. Wonderfully, he kissed her deeply, and she was lost. Wantonly, she pressed her breasts against his chest, needing the pressure.

Adam spread her legs but did not reach under her dress, nor did he remove any garment. He merely grazed his thumb along her inner thigh, and Ella felt her panties soak with the wetness already flowing from her. She prayed he would touch her where she needed satisfaction. But he did not.

Instead, Adam caressed her hips through the fabric wrapped around them. His grip felt possessive and adoring. Ella pressed back against the chair and spread her legs wider, begging him to take her. Lightly, he kissed her lips, and heat seared through her. With one finger he caressed just under her jaw.

Pushed beyond limits, Ella didn't know if she could resist coming. The more Adam touched her and teased her, the hotter she got. The desire to tear her clothes off, and his, was powerful. But she was mesmerized by his seduction and could do nothing but let him continue.

He ran his tongue over her lower lip and then grasped it in his teeth and tugged. Meanwhile, he held both her wrists, pressing her arms against the sides of the chair as if to restrain her. The feel of his dominance, of his tantalizing touches, was heady. Floating in a cloud of arousal, her clit tight as a pebble, Ella feared that she would soon have no strength to hold on.

And at that moment, that was exactly what happened. She felt Adam's breath against her cheek, his hands on her wrists, and a deep pulse throbbed between her legs. Almost before she knew what she was doing, she screamed low and deep. A heavy wave pounded through her body and she stiffened, every muscle tight and hard.

The orgasm washed over her, sweet and delicious, and she gasped with relief. Wave after wave convulsed through her sex, carrying her into a tender ecstasy. All the while, Adam held her wrists, but not tightly, just enough to feel what she felt. His face was so close to hers, she felt his hot breath throughout her release. It was as though he experienced it with her and took pleasure in her pleasure.

When at last she relaxed and collapsed against him, Adam just held her and stroked her hair. For a while, they stayed that way. When she had the strength, Ella raised her head and looked at him. Adam kissed her, and the touch was hot, needy. His desire aroused her all over again.

He lifted her into his arms and started toward the bedroom. Ella could feel his swollen erection pressed against her hip, and she wanted to be naked with him, needing nothing more than to give herself to him in every way she could think of. Some nights weren't meant for sleep. Especially when you were engaged and so much in love it hurt.

And that was one of those nights. Until the early hours of the morning, naked and alone together, Ella showed him how she felt. And Adam loved her back equally hard. They slept only when exhaustion finally took them and when they'd satisfied their craving for each other. At least for a little while.

Chapter 4

Since being with Adam, writing in her diary was less of a necessity for Ella. Still, when emotion surged it provided an outlet for her feelings. Sitting outside one day, she poured out her heart.

I keep pinching myself because I never thought I'd be this lucky. Adam is the sexiest man I've ever known—not that I've known many. But even if I had, I am sure he would top the list. The other night we stayed up all night making love. He is amazing, and I can't get enough of him.

The best part is that he wants me, too. I admit that's done a lot for my self-confidence. Though I still can't believe he chose me. Any woman would want him, and believe me I've seen them looking. But I am making an effort to live up to what he thinks of me.

Shopping has become a habit, and one I rather like. I am a girl, after all. And as I grew up there was always a need to be frugal. I think I still am cost conscious. But it's fun to be able to buy nice clothes that look good on me. And even better, clothes that turn Adam on.

We are going to be married soon but haven't set the date yet. We are not in a hurry. Just being together is enough. I am looking forward to the wedding, though.

I've dreamed of a special wedding since I was young, though for a long time I wasn't sure it would ever happen for me. And now it has. I love Adam with all my heart and soul.

And that's why I'm worried. Not about us. About his father. Yes, he is in Paraguay and Adam thinks there is a good chance he won't be back. The bad guys were annoyed over his betrayal and deception. Claudio successfully boxed himself into a corner. Now he's trapped and wouldn't dare return to Rio.

Then why do I worry? Maybe it's because I adore Adam so much. It's been a reprieve to have his father out of our life. But the peace and silence is unnerving, too. Like the calm before the storm. Which is why I am writing to you, my trusted diary. I need to get this off my mind.

I'm exaggerating the danger; I know I am. We are okay now and the future is bright. Adam won't let anything happen to me, or to us. He has assured me of that many times. And I believe him. I really do. But evil has a way of invading, even when it doesn't seem possible. It happened before. It could happen again.

I've just got to put this out of my mind and enjoy the present. My unfounded fears will only upset our life together. That's why I haven't told Adam. He doesn't need to know I have any concern, because he only wants to see me happy. So that's what I will give him. I'm strong enough to push aside my insecurities and give myself fully to our life together.

"Do you still write about me?"

Ella looked up to see Adam standing behind her.

"Sometimes." She smiled coyly. "But it's none of your business." Ella powered off her tablet and stood.

Adam pulled her into his arms. "Let's go shopping."

Ella raised her eyebrows. "You don't think I have enough clothes?"

He kissed her lips, and his eyes gleamed. "No, I don't.

You looked so sexy in that emerald-green dress."

Ella hugged him tighter. "Mmm, you did like that one, didn't you?"

"Yes." The look in his eyes confirmed what he said. "Let's go see what else we can find."

"I never thought men liked shopping."

"They do when they can watch the woman they crave model sexy clothes."

"Hmm, I imagine that does make a difference." Ella kissed his lips and started toward the hall. "Just let me get my purse. I wouldn't want to keep a sexy man in a shopping mood waiting."

Adam laughed a deep, masculine, joyful laugh as Ella disappeared around the corner.

*****

The weather turned even colder, but nothing happened to mar the tranquility of their time in Newport. On the contrary, Ella began to think that any anxiety she felt was irrational, so she forgot about it. The ongoing emails with Natalie Baker about the wedding dress design were enough to outshine any lesser concerns.

One day Ella got a call from Adam's sister. They didn't talk on the phone often, though they did text or email.

"Fiorella."

"Hello, Ella. It's so good to hear your voice."

"We should talk more often."

"I agree." Fiorella hesitated before going on. "That's why I couldn't resist calling. I have an idea, and I really hope you will like it."

"What? Tell me."

"December is coming up, and Christmas in Brazil is a big deal. I know you have family there, but I was hoping I could talk you into spending the holiday here."

"Oh, I'd love to. I've really missed Rio and I cannot wait to return. I'll check with Adam."

"Yes, that would be good. I would have mentioned it to him but I wanted to ask you first."

24

"I appreciate that. I guess it will just depend on his work, but I think he can do everything from Rio that he can do from here."

"Exactly. And there's something else."

"Sure." Ella was already excited at the prospect of returning to Brazil and seeing Adam's family again.

"I don't know how it is in America, but in Brazil any woman that gets engaged should have an engagement party. And I'd love to have a party for you, Ella. It's just something you shouldn't miss out on. Trust me, you are going to love it."

Ella didn't need to be convinced. She'd had enough experience in Rio to know that the Brazilians loved celebrations, and really knew how to do parties right. "That would be so amazing. I would love to have an engagement party." After she said it, Ella felt a bit awkward. Shyness surfaced when she least expected it, and the idea of being the center of attention was intimidating.

"It will be for the whole family. Weddings are important here, and it's good to give family a chance to celebrate."

That made Ella feel better. "Of course. Well, let me tell Adam. When are you thinking of doing the party?"

"It would be best before Christmas, say the middle of the month. If I start now, I'll have time to plan it."

"That's pretty soon. We should probably make plans to leave for Rio without too much delay. I'll see if Adam can work it out for us to be there within a couple of weeks."

"Perfect." Fiorella didn't hang up. "Oh, I nearly forgot to tell you. We met Tanner and Natalie."

"Really? When?"

"They were recently in Rio. It seems they came to Brazil for the São Paulo Fashion Week. Anyway, his attorney suggested Fiore's. He told them to try my restaurant if they were ever here, and they did."

"Wow, Fiorella. What were they like?"

"Very nice. Tanner is extremely handsome and self-assured. And Natalie was very friendly, easy to get to know. I think they enjoyed the food. I made some special dishes for them."

"Of course they liked the food. Everything you make is incredible."

"Ah, you flatter me. Anyway, I hope they will come back next time they are here. I get the impression they travel a lot. And I told Natalie that I'd seen the emails about your wedding dress, and that's it is lovely. She said it should be done soon."

"Yes, wait until you see the real thing, Fiorella. I am so glad I asked Natalie to create the design. I was timid to ask her, considering how well known she is. But like you said, she is so nice. She seemed to really want to create the dress for me. It's going to be special. I'll have to send her some wedding pictures so she can see me wearing it."

"I'm sure she would love that. So, talk to Adam. I'm sure he will want to be here over the holidays. Just nudge him to come earlier so we can have your engagement party."

"I'll let you know."

*****

It didn't take much convincing to get Adam to agree. He missed his family, and Brazil was still home to him. By early December, they returned to Rio. At first it was an adjustment to come from the winter temperatures in Newport Beach and go to the summer temperatures in Rio.

Summer in Rio started late November and lasted until March. So it was a shock the day they arrived to find it was eighty-five degrees and raining. And more rain was expected, as the highest precipitation in the city occurred during December.

But Ella didn't mind. The beaches would be packed with people over the holidays, and that was where she planned to be a lot of the time. Miguel picked them up at the airport, and Nico greeted them at home. It felt natural to be guarded; it was a dangerous city in many ways. The protection was a relief, as Ella didn't feel entirely safe, though there was nothing specific she could point to.

Fiorella had been preparing for the party for weeks, and everything was set. Adam and Ella had just enough time to settle back in and get used to Rio before the big night came. An engagement party is more a Brazilian tradition than American, and it was to be a memorable event.

In keeping with the spirit of celebration, Adam participated wholeheartedly, and Fiorella was thrilled to learn she could host the party at the Copacabana Palace, since he was paying the expenses. In Ella's mind, the whole thing seemed to have escalated out of control. But for Adam's sister, no party was elaborate enough.

The banquet hall looked sort of "beach renaissance" to Ella, a term she made up. The walls were a subdued gold with plaster columns sculpted into them, reminiscent of Roman times. The parquet flooring, floor-to-ceiling windows with embroidered satin drapes, and white fabric furniture next to glass-top tables gave the room a bold elegance.

Despite the classy ambience, Fiorella had only one purpose, and that was for everyone to have fun. Thus, formal wear was not part of the picture, but colorful clothes worn for dancing were. Ella wore a red one-shoulder dress with fringe along the bottom, and Fiorella chose a mint-green shimmery outfit. Spiked heels were expected, and all the time navigating a surfboard served Ella very well in balancing on the narrow support.

Adam's sister had gone all out in inviting friends and family; there were so many people that Ella had no hope of meeting them all or remembering them if she did. Instead, she stuck close to those few she knew. Adrian was never far from Fiorella, a sign of how much he adored his fiancée.

"Ciao," he said to Ella, kissing her three times, first on one cheek and then the other. "Are you getting the idea that Brazilians *live* to party?"

Looking at him decked out in black samba pants, full cut with a satin ribbon along the sides, and a bright green shirt, Ella once again thought of him as an Italian movie star. Thick brows over piercing gray eyes and his dark, wavy hair, slightly long, added to his sex appeal.

"Yes, I am getting that impression." Ella laughed.

Fiorella swooped up beside Adrian and wrapped her arm around him. She looked classically beautiful with her delicate features, her reddish-brown hair falling gently around her face. When Adrian squeezed her and kissed her cheek, her green eyes lit up.

"Where's Adam?" Fiorella asked, still holding tight to her love.

"He went to get us drinks."

At that moment, Adam reappeared with a drink in each hand. "Looking for me?"

If I wasn't, I sure would be now. Adam was devastatingly handsome in his shiny gold shirt and satin dance pants.

"What did you get me?" Ella took one of the drinks he offered.

"The bartender called it a tangerine-ginger caipirinha."

"Sounds lethal."

"It might be."

"I think we should dance," Ella said, eyeing the dance floor, which was rapidly filling up.

"We all should," Fiorella said, looking up at Adrian.

The drinks were left at their table, with Adam's mother to keep watch over them. Serena was all smiles, pleased as could be about her son's engagement. Dressed in a bright yellow dress, she looked ready to party. And she'd had the plastic surgery to fix the scar left from Claudio's last attack. With her thick, dark hair and classic bone structure, she was attractive, and the joy reflected in her face made her even more beautiful.

The samba was the most popular, and Ella decided the African-Brazilian dance was sexy. The clothes were sexy, the music, too. And the dance moves were decidedly so.

She'd learned not long before, but had practiced every time she'd gone out with Adam. Her confidence had built, and she thoroughly enjoyed it.

Everyone danced, even Adrian's parents, Bellina and Davi, who made a striking couple. Ella had met them before at a formal event and was glad to see them again. They'd been family friends for years, and now they'd be related when Adrian and Fiorella got married. Even Serena danced once things got going, and by all appearances had a great time.

Ella dragged Adam back to the table for a break. He seemed to have boundless energy, and was wearing her out. They held hands and smiled at each other, soaking in every minute of the memorable evening. To restore their energy, they ate their fill of canapés, tempura scallops, mushroom croquettes, and empanadas.

"Your sister arranged quite a menu." Ella took another bite of her croquette.

"It's not every day I marry such a special woman. I told Fiorella not to spare any cost."

"She understood that message." Ella laughed and looked at Adam's right hand.

It gave her pleasure to see his ring. Wanting to do everything Brazilian style, she'd put aside her diamond for the time being. In Brazil, the man and woman each wore a gold band on their right hand; Adrian and Fiorella wore them also. Inside was an inscription of the name of their betrothed. There was something so romantic about wearing such a ring.

Every time Ella looked at her own ring, she felt good, thinking of Adam's name inscribed in the gold. And when she saw the ring on his finger, it made her feel loved. On their wedding day, once they'd said their vows and were truly man and wife, they would move the rings to their left hands.

Later in the evening, champagne was poured and the music stopped. Adam and Ella stood next to Serena while she made a toast to the couple. Her heartfelt words were spoken in Portuguese, and Ella didn't know most of what she said. But all she had to do was look at his mother's expression to understand the message. She ended, eyes filled with tears, by saying "Parabéns." It was the one word Ella understood: *Congratulations.*

Hugs and excitement were in no short supply. Fiorella stood with Adrian and followed Serena's toast with one of their own. The crowd seemed swept up into the celebratory spirit, and numerous other toasts followed from people Ella didn't know. Everything was in Portuguese, but the sentiment didn't need to be translated. When the enthusiasm ebbed, the music started up again and the crowd hit the dance floor with verve.

Ella was a little overwhelmed by all the excitement and effusive affection. In some ways it was difficult for her to be comfortable in such a friendly, festive environment. But she tried her best. And she was very touched that Fiorella had made her engagement to Adam such an event. She couldn't think of a way to thank her enough. But then, to Adam's sister, having such a party was likely all the reward she looked for.

Chapter 5

The dancing lasted well past midnight, but Adam felt energized by it. And by Ella's nearness to him. She was the embodiment of sexuality, with her slender curves, tanned, lean legs, and long mane of brown hair. The entire evening, all he could think about was being alone with her, and having her.

They danced together, one song after the other. Watching her samba—her hips swaying and her lovely legs kicking—drove Adam crazy. Every move, every touch, was a sensual tease, fueling his need for her. The party had been packed with guests, some he knew, and many he didn't. Not long into the festivities, he had eyes only for his fiancée, and she only for him. They were in a world of their own, bounded by their love and commitment to each other.

Once they were back at the beach house, Adam stepped out to the patio and the warm night air hit him. It was humid and sensual, only adding to his excitement. The city lights glimmered across the bay and the night sky was like a heavenly dome above.

He pulled his love into his arms and smelled the exotic aroma of her perfume mixed with the delicate body fragrance that was uniquely Ella.

"Do you feel engaged?" He ran his thumb over her

lower lip.

She looked directly at him, burning into his soul.

"Yes. Very much so." Ella bit his thumb playfully.

He pressed her luscious body against his; the arousal he felt was no secret.

"I want you...so much. I want you to be my wife."

Adam kissed her, tasting her sweetness and relishing the softness of her lips. Dipping his tongue against hers, he felt her love in return, and his arousal grew. Delving into her mouth, wanting to feel every part, he kissed deeply. *Ella, sweet Ella.*

He stepped back and looked at her. The glisten of her skin in the patio light and the glazed look of desire in her eyes pushed him a bit too close for comfort. But he couldn't resist.

"Take your panties off. But leave the dress on."

Adam watched intently as she slipped off her heels and then reached up under the red dress. The way she moved and the sensual act of reaching under the hem to find her panties and pull them to her ankles was riveting. Ella didn't realize her sexuality, not fully. It was another thing that made her impossibly attractive.

The passion within her could not be contained; that Adam knew from experience. And the anticipation of what was to come titillated him. Watching her, and following every tiny movement, he saw her slip the panties down her thighs and let them drop to her ankles.

She stepped out of them and stood before him, vulnerable, naked under the flimsy dress. Her brown eyes were large, her own desire evident. And her lips parted, inviting him to her. As his gaze drifted down, he saw her nipples poking against the fabric still covering them.

Adam kicked off his shoes and slipped off his shiny shirt, allowing her to drink in the sight of his bare, muscled chest. Knowing she liked it, and that his buff chest, shoulders, and arms turned her on, he let her look. There was no reaction except in her eyes. There he saw all.

"I like you naked." Adam didn't need to imagine her

bare under the dress as he had all evening. She was naked, though covered in the red stretchy fabric, barely.

Adam took one step to close the gap between them and dropped to his knees in front of her. Holding her hips, he leaned in and kissed her sex through the red material, feeling electricity from the touch. He dropped his hands behind her and squeezed her tight ass.

Ella fingered his hair, her fingertips alive with desire. Adam touched her thighs, and, looking into her eyes, he let his hands drift up until they were under the hem of her skirt. He could see her hold her breath for a moment then release it.

He reached higher, touching her flat belly with his palms, careful not to graze her most sensitive areas. Without exploring, he knew she was wet. Just her look conveyed the intensity of her feeling. Running his hands across her flat belly, Adam felt his erection swell.

Slowly, he moved his hands down. Ella panted softly. He stopped at the top of her thighs, knowing that with a small movement he could touch her where she wanted him to. Yet he didn't, only watched her. The piercing look she gave him was like a tender stroke to his heated erection.

Unwilling to look away, Adam held her gaze and took the liberty of pressing one hand over her mons. Ella whimpered.

"Amore mia," he whispered.

Ella licked her lips and swallowed. Knowing she was balanced on a fine precipice, Adam took advantage. He let one hand slip between her legs and reach behind to cup her ass. With his other hand, he dipped into her wet slit, making her gasp.

"I want you," he whispered. Ella's panting was louder. The soft roll of the surf beyond the patio rail was in harmony with her feminine sound.

Losing his fingers in her sweet cream, Adam swirled it around and Ella arched her back slightly. Squeezing her buttocks and holding her firm, he proceeded to play with her pussy. Each movement created a reaction that he saw flicker in her eyes. And each time, his cock got harder.

Deftly, he slid two fingers inside her, and Ella quivered.

"Yes," he whispered. "You are mine. You will give me your pleasure."

Stroking in and out with his fingers, he felt Ella relax into him, beckoning for more. Plunged inside her, Adam tapped over her clit with his thumb, and she moaned.

"Oh God." Ella half closed her eyes.

Enthralled with her stimulation, Adam moved his fingers a little faster and pressed his thumb a fraction deeper to flick over her clit. Her panting was fast and erratic. Watching her pushed Adam's own arousal higher.

"Don't hold it back," he said, the sound of his own voice coming from deep in his throat.

Adam increased the speed and pressure of his movements and Ella made a guttural sound in the back of her throat. Then her body went stiff, and he could feel the convulsions from deep in her sex. Her strong inner muscles clenched around his fingers and she trembled as the waves of pleasure took her.

After a few moments, she relaxed and Adam stood. He held her in his arms and kissed her sweetly, loving the submission he felt in her. Adam reached down, grabbed the hem of the dress, and pulled it off over her head. Then he undid the see-through mesh bra and tossed it aside. Seeing Ella completely naked made his cock drip. He could feel his pants getting wet.

She reached out and pulled down his loose dance pants so he could kick them away. After hesitating only a moment to look at the bulge in his shorts, Ella reached inside and cupped his balls. Adam moaned loudly.

Softly she squeezed, and then grasped the base of his stalk. The feeling was too amazing and pre-cum seeped out the top, wetting the rim of his shorts. Ella smeared it around with her finger then pulled his underwear all the way off.

Lightly, she teased his cock with her fingertips, making

it jerk with pleasure.

"I love you, Adam," she whispered, staring at his thick erection.

Adam lifted her in his arms and carried her to a padded lounge chair. He positioned her against the back, which was partially lowered. He spread her legs and kneeled between them. Leaning over her, he blew on her wet pussy, watching her squirm.

Then he cupped her firm breasts, massaging them sensually before kissing her taut nipples. Adam swirled his tongue over the creamy crests and then bit her distended nipples. Ella gripped his shoulders, her breathing ragged.

"I want you so bad," she gasped.

Leaning back, knees still bent, Adam let her look at his swollen cock. Her eyes on him sent warm heat through his body, as though she'd touched his skin.

"I want you now." Ella's pleading tone melted all resistance.

Adam had to have her.

Gripping his cock at the base, he angled toward her hot pussy. The thick knob dipped through her outer lips and her warmth caressed him. He lifted her hips so she was on top of his knees. Ella was still on her back, her sex lifted onto his lap.

Gently, he eased into her. Ella was so wet that he slid without effort, and she pushed her hips up to assist his entry. Deeper and deeper he went, her soft heat stretching around him. When he was as deep as he could go, he leaned back, supporting his weight with one arm behind him. With the other, he pressed down on Ella's vulva.

She gasped, and a light convulsion of her inner muscles teased his cock.

"You're so big," she whispered. "So wide...I love how you fill me up."

Her words pushed him close to release. Looking at Ella on her back, her thick hair wild around her, Adam felt an intensity of emotion he wasn't sure he could handle. Her pussy was on his lap, his burning cock buried inside her.

And something about the angle with him sitting on his knees, leaned back, made it all the more erotic.

"Tell me you are mine." Adam wanted to hear her say it. He was going to take her, but he wanted to hear the words from her own lips.

"I am yours, Adam," she gasped. "I'll always be yours."

Rocking his hips, Adam fucked her, deep and hard. The sound of Ella's soft moans and panting edged him past any shred of control. Then he felt her convulse around his aching cock and felt her body stiffen. As she was propelled into another orgasm, Adam fell into his own release. His body turned to steel, and his cock spurted with such power it ached.

Then it felt so good. As he released into the woman he loved, Adam witnessed her ecstasy, and together they ascended into a state of ultimate pleasure. He felt one with her, as if there was no boundary separating his pleasure from hers. The two merged and blended, making each more exhilarating that it would ever have been alone.

When they relaxed, Adam pulled her into his arms and held her like the treasure she was. He wanted to tell her just how much he really loved her, and what she meant to him. But there were no words to express what he felt at that moment. All he could do was hold her, swamped with the depth of emotion Ella had stirred within him.

Unwilling for the night or the moment to end, Adam cleaned them off with a pool towel then guided Ella to the beach. It was only a few steps down from the patio. He got two fresh towels, one for each of them to wrap around their nakedness, and followed the path to the shoreline.

It was a private beach. And even though Adam knew his security would keep an eye on them, he didn't care. He just wanted to be out in nature with Ella. The moon was full, the huge amber orb bright with the statue of Christ the Redeemer high above, silhouetted by its light. At the water's edge, Adam spread each of their towels on the sand. He dropped down to his and reached for Ella.

There, under the gleaming Brazilian night sky, they

stretched out on their backs, naked. It was Rio, and nudity was more accepted than it was in Newport. Looking up at the endless dark expanse above them, and holding Ella's hand, was a moment Adam would never forget. The water lapped against the shore, and the warm night air settled over them.

"Amore mia," he whispered, the simple endearment like poetry on his lips.

Ella turned her head to look at him.

"I love you." She mouthed the words slowly and silently.

Adam's heart surged with joy. He wasn't sure any man had a right to be as happy as he was right then. But he seized the opportunity. He would love Ella forever, and do everything he could to protect and honor her. Adam lifted her hand and pressed it to his lips, then looked back at the endless night sky.

Chapter 6

Christmas was already in the air in Rio, with decorations in the major shopping centers, and Santas called *Papai Noels* appearing in full traditional costumes. In many ways the holiday was much like Ella had experienced in California, but the tropical heat did seem a bit out of place. The celebration of food, family, lights, and gift giving was done in Brazilian style.

Zona Sul—or the south zone of Rio, where tourists usually stayed—housed many hotels around a lagoon. Mostly known as Lagoa, it was famous for the largest floating Christmas tree in the world. Nearly 279 feet tall, it sat atop the lagoon, where it would stay throughout the holidays.

People gathered in the rain to watch the annual lighting of the tree and watch a fireworks display to usher in the season. Ella was not there for that part, but later when she went with Adam's family to see the tree, she was amazed by the lights, reflectors, and strobe effects. The brightly lit tree changed colors from blue, red, orange, and green, creating four different scenes, while circling the lagoon on a constant loop.

Adam told her the late-night mass at the church had lost popularity due to the high crime rate. But Ella attended church with the family on Christmas Eve in the afternoon. The big meal was planned for late in the day; it was traditionally eaten around midnight. The occasion was celebrated at the Bianci family home, and the women worked together in the kitchen, preparing the feast. Adrian stopped by to be with Fiorella for a while, and later went to eat with his parents.

With Serena's experience with traditional food, and Fiorella's gourmet expertise, everything came out superbly. Ella was glad she could assist, though she mostly watched the other two work their magic in the kitchen while sipping her caiparinha. Initially, she'd found the drink too strong, but being in Rio she'd acclimated to it, and quite liked it.

Christmas dinner was a large spread of roast turkey, ham, rice, salad, and kale highly seasoned with garlic. The turkey was the centerpiece, but in true Brazilian fashion it was served with local exotic fruits. Ella's favorite was the dessert called *rabanada*, a dish that reminded her of French toast. Thick slices of day-old bread were dipped in a mixture of milk and beaten eggs, fried in butter, then covered in thick syrup made from port, honey, and cinnamon.

Gifts were a part of the celebration, though they didn't seem to hold the same importance as they had in Ella's experience. The family being together, church, and the cozy meal made the day what it was. And the city was alive with festivity. Huge Christmas trees composed of colored lights could be seen against the night sky. It was dramatic, and Ella could not help but be in the spirit of the season.

After the late meal, it was traditional to sleep in the next morning. And there was one tradition that could only take place in warmer climates. Many families headed to the beach to celebrate their Christmas Day in the sun, as did the Biancis. And that suited Ella just fine. Soaking up the sun, she thought of her own family. Though they were invited to Brazil, neither her mother or her sister wanted to spend the holiday away from California.

They felt more comfortable with what they were used

to, so they had declined despite Adam's generous offer to pay their way. Christmas had never been a big deal when Ella grew up, as her family was never close. And her mother was staying with Margie, so it made sense for them to celebrate together, considering they were both single and alone. Julianna had said she'd drive up to see their mother on Christmas Day.

*****

The celebration of New Year's Eve in Rio was second only to the world-renowned Carnival later in the year. Ella enjoyed dinner that evening at Cipriani with Adam, Fiorella, and Adrian. She learned the restaurant had been one of the top choices for Northern Italian cuisine for over twenty years. The décor, including white drapes, linen table cloths, and watercolors depicting Venice scenes, created a Venetian flair.

"It's so romantic here," Fiorella said, leaning into Adrian. She wore a white dress with a pearl necklace, and her fiancé wore a white shirt.

Ella had also worn white, and matched Adam in his white linen shirt. "I agree, it's very romantic. I'm not sure I look good in white, though."

"It's good luck. Everybody wears it for the New Year's celebration. And it looks great with your blue garnets."

Ella fingered the necklace Adam had given to her as a gift. She loved it because it reminded her of the ocean. "I'm for good luck."

Adam smiled and wrapped his arm around her. "You look lovely. The white looks good with your tan."

Never tiring of Adam's flattery, she smiled back.

The restaurant was on the ground floor of the Copacabana and had a view of the pool, lit up for the evening. Adam had secured a table by the windows. It was cozy in the red velvet seats, listening to the live piano music playing in the background.

"I've been here a couple of times, and I think you will enjoy the food. The chef has a contemporary slant on

Italian dishes, but he seems to know what we prefer, here in Brazil." Holding his menu, Adam began to scan the choices.

"You may have to help me decide." Ella looked at the plethora of items offered. "I am so hungry that everything looks good."

"Me too," Adrian said. "I played soccer today, which really worked up an appetite."

"I'm going to try this," Fiorella said, pointing to it as she read. "Lobster risotto with lemon."

"Since we are all so starved, I'll order the carpaccio and truffles for appetizers." Adam flagged the waiter, who appeared within seconds, and the order was placed.

"Any questions I can answer for you?" The waiter in a white shirt and black pants with a linen towel over one arm looked ready to serve.

"Yes." Ella lifted her hand. "What is saltimbocca?"

"Ah, yes, an excellent dish. Chicken is pounded flat and thinly wrapped in prosciutto. Sage leaves are added, and it's marinated in the chef's own herb blend, then sautéed. In Italian, the word saltimbocca means 'to jump in the mouth,' which gives you the idea that the dish is so good it literally jumps into your mouth."

"Yum. Well, when we order I think I'll have that." Ella leaned back in her chair.

"Good choice," Adrian chimed in. "If it's anything like the one Fiorella makes, you will enjoy it."

"Except I make mine with veal," Fiorella added.

Having studied the list of Italian wines, Adam made a suggestion. "How about this La Spinetta 2009 Sangiovese Tuscany?"

Everyone nodded, and the waiter gave a half-bow before leaving to get the wine for them. Fortunately, the appetizers arrived quickly, helping to take the edge off hunger. Decisions were made and orders placed. Adam picked the green tagliarini with ham and cheese gratin, and Adrian the ossobusso—*veal shanks braised with vegetables,* the menu said.

The ladies had already made their choices. While waiting for the main courses, they all sipped their wine. Adrian began chatting with Adam about his soccer game, losing the attention of the women.

Fiorella shrugged. "Let them talk about sports. I have something else I want to talk to you about."

Ella put her wine glass down. "Sure."

"Well, Adrian and I were talking about our wedding date. We always wanted it to be in the spring, and the spring season is short here, only April and May. Anyway, the other night we discussed it, and decided late April would be the best."

"That sounds wonderful."

"It's beautiful here then. It would allow enough time to get the invitations out, and do all the planning." Fiorella paused and got a big grin.

"What?" Ella knew there was something more.

"Well, we had an idea. What if we made it a double wedding?"

Ella felt the excitement.

"You and Adam could get married the same day. It would be one huge celebration."

"Wow, that's actually a great idea."

"What? Did I hear something about a wedding?" Adam ceased his conversation with Adrian and directed his question to his sister.

"Yes. What do you think, Adam? Wouldn't it be wonderful to get married on the same day?" Fiorella looked so pleased with the idea that Ella couldn't imagine her older brother refusing her.

"What do you think?" Adam looked at Ella, revealing nothing.

"I like the idea. It would be amazing doing it together...as long as that's what everybody wants." Ella squeezed Adam's hand.

"I like it, too." Adam leaned over and kissed Ella.

"Okay, then, that's everybody." Adrian lifted his glass to toast. "A double wedding in April."

The glasses clinked as each toasted.

"And my dress can be ready by then. Before we left Newport, the final design was sent. Natalie finished it, so all I have to do is have it constructed."

"You can use the same lady who is making mine." Fiorella took another sip of her wine.

"Now I'm really excited." Ella looked at Adam again. "You aren't going to get cold feet, are you?"

Adam laughed. "Not a chance. I can't wait."

The meals were served and were every bit as tasty as expected. The aromas wafted up, reminding Ella of how hungry she still was.

"No wonder I'm so hungry," she said, cutting her chicken to take a bite. "It's after ten thirty. We never eat this late."

"Well, enjoy. There's plenty of time for dessert, too. The fireworks won't start for a while. We can go up to the roof in about an hour and join the party up there to wait," Adam said.

Ella nodded, her mouth too full for her to speak. Watching the others eat with relish, she realized they were as hungry as she was. It was fun, though, going out late and partying. Especially with those she loved so much. After spending time with them over the last few weeks, Ella really felt like part of the family. And soon she would be for real, as Adam's new wife.

By the time they made it through the chocolate almond cake, which had to be almost pure chocolate, Ella was stuffed. It was very rich but melted in her mouth, and she ate every last bite. Leisurely, they sipped espressos then made their way to the party. On the roof was a heated swimming pool, a gym, and a bar serving drinks and snacks.

Champagne was flowing, so that was what they ordered. The place was packed but they made their way out to the railing to get a better look at the breathtaking view of Copacabana Beach and Sugarloaf beyond it. The weather was warm and a little drizzly.

Stages were set along the beach with live music shows that had been going on for hours. Ella could hear Brazilian tunes, which many danced to. The area was wall-to-wall people waiting for the fireworks. They were all dressed in white, and some were throwing flowers into the water.

"Why do they do that?" Ella asked.

"It is an offering to Yemanja, the deity of the seas. It's a party to thank her for her blessings." Fiorella gazed out over the packed shoreline.

"I'm glad we are up here. I wouldn't want to fight that crowd." Ella was still amazed at how many people came to celebrate. She could hear the yelling and shouting of the partiers below.

"Yes, it's safer up here. But it's not too bad down there, really. You just can't bring anything with you. There are lots of pickpockets."

Adrian put his arm around Fiorella, distracting her from the conversation.

"This is going to be a good year for us, amore mia." Adam held Ella's hand to his cheek. "You will be my wife."

"Nothing will make me happier." Ella leaned over and kissed Adam, loving his taste.

The show started with a boom. The midnight display was worth waiting for. The fireworks stations were in boats anchored a distance from shore. Though the bands along the beach continued to play their music, the explosions above the water drowned them out. In the distance, when the sky lit up, Ella could see cruise ships farther out. Their passengers were enjoying the view from the decks.

When the first flares of red hit the sky, the crowd began to scream. The dull roar of their excitement exploded along with the fireworks. Brilliant flashes of white and yellow hit the dark sky and popped in a rapid staccato as they dispersed into shards of light. The atmosphere over the bay shone with blinding amber and white. Then it turned to sparkling glitter, just before huge balls of light blossomed into the image of glowing dandelion flowers.

Orbs of purple, orange, and red, exploded faster and faster. The noise echoed like rapid popgun sounds. The show wowed the crowd with the flashes of light like diamonds bursting apart and flowers of color propelled into the night. The performance continued for at least twenty minutes, and all the while, the audience never stopped screaming and shouting.

In fact, the noise level got louder as things progressed. And deep in the masses, some started whistling in admiration. Then the sky turned white and glowing confetti drifted down like mini asteroids. Just before the end, the night turned brilliant red like a raging fire then went black, before the next round of rainbow-hued rockets. Huge white bursts held, suspended in the air, then plunged forward as if they'd reach the hotel rooftop, but faded before they did.

Ella was laughing and screeching along with the mob on the rooftop. She glanced over to see that Fiorella and Adrian were doing the same. It was liberating, and definitely Ella's best New Year's Eve. She caught sight of Adam laughing, and running his hand through his hair with exuberance. His joy magnified hers. It was definitely going to be a good year. And she was really going to get married.

*****

Planning for the April wedding started immediately after the new year. Normally, engaged couples in Brazil waited a long time before the wedding. But Fiorella had known Adrian most of her life; they were childhood sweethearts. She had no patience for waiting. And Ella was from California and had no such tradition.

The preparations were extensive. And everyone they knew was coming. Even Kaiyla and Steve were flying over for the week, along with Ella's mother and sister. Quinn, the attorney Adam trusted as much as any friend, was attending with his girlfriend, Tia. Plus, there was a whole list of people culled from the rest of Adam's staff.

Bad feelings toward Violetta, the woman who had previously sought Adam's affection, had long since been put aside, so she was invited, along with Vitto, who still adored her. Then there was all the family, including Serena and Adrian's mother and father. And a long list of cousins and relatives that even Fiorella didn't know that well. Nonetheless, they were all invited. The invitation list grew and grew, but no one seemed concerned about it.

Adam was marrying the woman he loved and any extravagance was permissible. Adding to how important the day was already, his younger sister was getting married at the same time. It was a day they would all remember and treasure forever. Thankfully, wedding planners and organizers were hired to assist with all the details. Even Fiorella, in her zest for celebrations, couldn't have handled it alone.

And Ella felt a bit lost. She'd never been to such a big wedding, much less prepared for one. Decisions about flowers, cake, and assorted issues seemed endless. But it was all fun. In Brazil, things were much more relaxed than they would have been in California. Attendees weren't expected to come in expensive garb. Sure, they all dressed up, but they came in whatever they had or could borrow.

It was all about the party, and about witnessing the commitment of love between the bride and groom. In this case brides and grooms. Ella's priority was her wedding dress, since she'd put a lot of planning into its creation. The seamstress was doing a quality job of constructing the dress. A few weeks ahead, a fitting was arranged.

They went together, and Fiorella tried on her own dress for the first time, too. At only five feet three, and small boned, she needed something that wouldn't overpower her. The competent Brazilian seamstress had catered to her needs and sewn a strapless satin dress that wrapped around the figure to below the knee, accenting the waist. Then it flared out at the bottom. Over the bodice and in a band, angled across the hips, were pearls embedded into the fabric.

"It's stunning," Ella said when she saw Fiorella spin around in front of the mirror. The single strand of pearls she wore with it was delicate and the ideal accent for the dress.

"I think so, too. I love it." She swiveled her hips to see the flared fabric from knee to hem move with her. Then she turned to look at Ella. "*That* dress was made for you."

Ella giggled. "Actually, it was."

She looked in the mirror, admiring how the dress fit her slender curves and showed off her figure in the best way. Rhinestones were encrusted along the top of the bodice, and the fabric swept across her body and gathered at the left hip, where more gems were cast. Then the dress skimmed down to the ankle with no excess fabric. It was soft and feminine, but didn't have extra ruffles or frills. The design was exactly what Ella had asked for.

"It's elegant." Fiorella stepped over to get a closer look. "The gems really set it off. And the diamond pendant necklace is a good choice."

"Now all we need is shoes."

"And I know just the place. In Brazil, the bride wears gold shoes."

"I want to do it all the Brazilian way." Ella smiled at her soon-to-be sister-in-law. "This is fun."

Chapter 7

The week before the wedding, Adam had come in from the pool, missing Ella. She had gone shopping with his sister and was enjoying every minute, he was sure. He'd worked as long as he could but had been unable to put her out of his mind. He loved her so much, and soon they would be married.

Now, he sat at his desk, staring at the vile message, his half-empty coconut drink pushed aside. The letter, not even typed but composed of cutout magazine letters, looked absurd. Adam had lost track of time after calling Nico to alert him to the new risk to their safety. He didn't know how long he'd been sitting there with the irrational hope that maybe the threat would just disappear.

But it didn't. Unmoving, he stared at the message, knowing it was a command to turn over some unspecified sum of money. Adam almost wouldn't mind that if it would ensure the safety of his family and his new wife to be. But he knew it wouldn't. The words *You will never see Ella again* stung. Nothing was more precious to him than Ella.

"Adam?"

He hadn't heard her come in.

Ella walked over to the desk. "What is it? Nico just said we had to come home right away. Something about 'plans have changed,' but I didn't understand."

Adam didn't say anything, unable to face telling his love the news.

"Adam?" She walked around the desk and put her hand on his shoulder. "What is it?"

She looked so beautiful, so innocent, and it broke Adam's heart to have to tell her of the threat. Ella didn't deserve it. A pang of guilt stabbed his chest for bringing her into his life. Any peace he attained never seemed to last. Yet, on the heels of that unwelcome emotion, he felt anger. Adam resented his father intruding into their happiness and he would not tolerate it.

Ella glanced at the letter on the desk. "Why is it written like that, in cutout letters?"

"Because it is from a criminal who doesn't want his threats traced."

"Who?"

Adam just looked at her.

"No. Not Claudio." Ella covered her mouth with her hand. "Adam...he can't be back. How could he get back?"

Adam shook his head. "I don't think he is here. But I do think he has managed to find an ally, maybe more than one. Someone had to post this letter from Rio. So that means if Claudio is not here, then his accomplice is."

"What does he want?"

"Money. Of course." Adam leaned back in his chair. "Only this time he doesn't just want software he can profit from. No. He doesn't want to work at all. Claudio just wants me to *give* him money."

"How much?"

"The letter doesn't say, just that I'll be contacted with the details of the demand."

"And what if you don't pay?"

Adam froze.

"What? What does the letter say?"

"It says, 'If you don't pay, you will never see Ella again.'"

"Oh my God."

Adam pulled Ella onto his lap and hugged her protectively. She clung to him.

"I will not let them touch you. I won't. There has to be a way to thwart him. I'll step up security for now. For all we know it's an idle threat. Though I doubt it. But when I find out how much money he wants, we will figure out what to do. Until he contacts me again, I have time to plan. We out-maneuvered him before. We can do it again."

Ella stood, and Adam got up from his chair and went to the window. He said nothing for a minute.

"Adam...I can't believe it. Our wedding is only a week away. Why now? Why do this at all?"

Still looking out at the water as if a solution could be found there, Adam answered.

"He knows I have money. Greed, that's what it is. He will risk everything to get to the money."

"What are we going to do?"

Turning to look at her, Adam took a deep breath. "For now, I think it's best if we don't share this information with anyone. It won't help for the family to know. I'll meet with Nico right away and lock down security. They won't get to us. And then we will wait for the demand. *If* it ever comes."

"I agree. It would only frighten Fiorella. And heavens, my mother and sister wouldn't know what to think. We will protect them. I'm not afraid of your father. The man is a coward. All he can do is bully people. He won't get away with it."

"No. He won't."

As if recalling the risk that Ella could be taken from him, Adam walked back to her and pulled her into a secure embrace.

Ella pressed her cheek against his chest. "I thought he had made so many enemies here that his life was at risk."

Adam leaned back to look into her eyes. "Yes, that is the case. But I've spoken to Taiz, and since we have been doing business together he has seemed willing to be forthright with me. He says Claudio wasn't worth going after. That he is a cheap criminal and poses no threat from Paraguay. However, Taiz told me Claudio wouldn't dare return to Rio."

"Maybe your father isn't a threat to Taiz from Paraguay, but he clearly has not changed his ways."

Adam shook his head. "No, he hasn't. And I don't think he ever will. Like an errant child, if he thinks he can get away with something, he will."

"Except he is dangerous."

Sitting on the top of his desk, Adam pulled Ella to him, wrapping his arms around her waist to keep her close. He considered what she'd just said.

"Claudio would like to think so, but cowards are never strong. We just need to find his weak point. When he left Rio, his gambling debts to Taiz were huge. If he ever does get money, repayment would be expected. I don't know what he hopes to achieve by stirring up bad feelings."

"Yes, you would think he'd want to stay off the radar."

"True. Which is one thing that doesn't quite make sense. But he is likely desperate. Even if he escaped the gambling debts temporarily, my father is still broke. He will always be broke, because whatever money comes into his hands, he spends on drugs."

"It's a never-ending cycle."

"Very much. And if it didn't involve us, I could just look the other way. Now he has brought you back into his vicious plans. He must know Taiz is still an ally. It seems foolhardy to risk his ire, as Taiz is loyal. It's not his responsibility to protect you or me, but I know he would not take kindly to harm befalling us."

"You would think Claudio would have considered that."

"That's the thing. High on drugs and crazy anyway, the man doesn't think rationally. He is in an untenable position and he is unpredictable. He always has been."

Ella wrapped her arms around Adam's neck and pressed her cheek against his neck.

"He has made too many enemies. Your father can't succeed. Any gain would be temporary."

"You and I know that. But in his fight for survival, he's not considering consequences. If he was, Claudio would not have written this letter. I would not have predicted this kind of boldness from him. But you never know."

Ella didn't seem anxious to leave Adam's lap. Despite her brave reaction, he knew the situation was frightening.

"I've already informed Nico about the letter, so he will take action to tighten our protection. I know he is already doing so. I'll get briefed by him later. He's trained for this job; he will know what to do."

Right then, the only thing Adam wanted to do was be with Ella. He held her in his arms and he never wanted to let her go, unable to face the possibility of losing her. His efforts to reassure the woman he loved that no harm would come to her only went so far. Of all people, Ella knew that evil, by nature, had a way of attacking when least expected.

*****

Ella sat in Adam's lap with her arms around his neck. If only she never had to let him go. If only his father had really disappeared for good. The reality was that he hadn't. And now he'd surfaced with a new threat. One directed at her. Despite the tentacle of fear that pressed into her consciousness, she didn't want to let Adam see it.

He would be worried enough. Knowing she was frightened would only make it more difficult. Adam would do everything he could to protect her, and they had resources to fuel that protection. And many allies. So why was she nervous about it?

The house was secure. Several members of Nico's team guarded them at all times, no matter where they were. Often, Ella forgot they were present, as they'd become a part of her everyday existence. And the perimeter of the property had motion detectors so no one could get past without setting off an alarm.

For the moment, Ella knew she was safe. Yet they couldn't stay hidden away in the beach house, not with their wedding a week away. And her family was arriving soon. There was never a good time for danger, but it seemed Claudio had picked one of the worst times. Despite the gloom that surrounded them, Ella was determined to be strong.

Once Adam released her from his lap, they went to have a beer before dinner. Something to relax. Right then there was nothing they could do about the pressing issue. They had to stay calm and respond with a clear head when the time came. Eli, the German chef who had been with Adam for years, made dinner for them.

Ella had little appetite, and Adam didn't either, it seemed. Guiltily, they left the barely touched plates at the table and went out on the patio to look across the bay. The tranquility of the ocean was soothing. The chef cleaned up and departed, leaving them alone, except for the personal guards discreetly looking out for them.

The sun had set but light played in the sky from the city lights decorating the shoreline. Taking her hand, Adam led her inside and up to the bedroom. Without a word, he began undoing the buttons of her blouse, making Ella weak with desire. The mood was subdued but the strength of their need was great.

After opening her blouse, Adam reached behind and undid her bra then reached under the satin to cup her breasts. She whimpered when he squeezed. The thought of separation from him, not knowing what might happen, increased her longing. A deep, potent feeling coursed through her.

Hotly, he placed his mouth over hers, kissing deeply. And Ella responded, accepting him. She rubbed her tongue next to his in wanton need. The taste of him and his warmth escalated the wondrous feeling overtaking her.

Dropping to her knees, Ella undid his board shorts and let them fall to the ground. Then she reached inside his cotton briefs, the heat of his cock burning to the touch, and felt his erection. He was so virile and masculine. With his thighs lean from surfing, his abdomen hard and flat, he was sculpted for her pleasure.

Reaching lower, Ella cupped his tight balls, rolling them in her hand. When Adam moaned, she yanked down his shorts, baring him for full access. His cock, swollen with desire, sprang free. Teasingly, she brushed her fingertips along the sides, loving the sight of the bulging veins.

At the thick knob, Ella ran her palm over it, smearing the pre-cum around. Then she put her mouth over the top, and Adam moaned. The smell of him, the maleness, and the scent of sex was a potent aphrodisiac. God, she could never get enough of him. Sucking gently, she felt as though he'd allowed her past some unseen barrier.

Having her mouth on him so intimately was a privilege only for her. Lowering over his stiff member, Ella pressed her lips on his velvet skin, closing her eyes to let the enjoyment seep in. Breathing in as she pumped up and down slowly over his cock, the dizzying aroma of his arousal fueled her own.

Letting him pop out of her mouth, Ella stroked her tongue up his cock and looked into his glazed-over eyes. Fingering his golden pubic hair, she felt so much love she thought she'd burst. Adam had his fingers in her hair, and looking at him, all she wanted was his pleasure. The pleasure only she could give him.

Reaching behind and grabbing his rock-hard ass, Ella covered his thick knob with her lips and sucked. Adam's heavy panting sped up, and the power she had over him was exhilarating. The more he reacted to her ministrations, the more it turned her on. Dropping her head over him, Ella took more of his length and put pressure along his shaft as she slid down.

Adam moaned loudly, and Ella increased her speed, wanting everything from him. His cock swelled in her mouth and she sucked harder. With one hand she cupped his hot balls, letting one finger slip behind to caress the tender strip between his legs. Faster and faster he panted, and his moans became louder.

Taking in every delicious taste of him, Ella gave in to her urge. She wanted to smell him, taste him, and feel him in her mouth. The bulge of his cock against her lips had her wet and needy. Sucking and licking, she showed no mercy, and Adam groaned a painful, sexual sound. Then he spurted in her mouth.

Ella squeezed his balls and took all the cum he gave her. It tasted salty and sensual. His body stiffened, with his muscles like steel and his belly tight. She swallowed what he gave her, and it felt like she was accepting an intimate gift, something no one else could have. Something highly erotic.

When Adam came over the crest of his orgasm, he pulled Ella up into his arms and kissed her. He swirled his tongue inside her mouth, tasting his own flavor. The kiss was deep and loving. She kissed back, pressing against his lips, aware of her tight clit and the moisture between her legs.

After quickly undressing both of them, Adam fell back on the bed with her on top of him. The look on his face was soft and satisfied. He brushed her long hair back over her shoulder and pulled her to him for another kiss. Ella's nipples were like little pebbles grazing against his rock-hard chest. Every touch sent electricity through her.

Kissing was as erotic as everything else. The more Adam kissed her, the weaker she felt in his arms, and more her clit begged for pressure. Impulsively, she straddled him and rubbed her pussy on his cock. It felt so good and she needed it so much. Unembarrassed, she stroked her wet slit over his cock, which got hard in response to her motion.

He was ready for her again. Raising up on her knees and straddling his hips, Ella fisted his erection, and Adam made a deep, guttural sound in his throat. Panting, her breathing ragged, Ella touched his thick knob to her wet opening. An electric sensation warmed her, deep in her core. She raked the tip of his cock over her clit several times, but it brought her too close to release and she moved it away.

Adam reached up and flicked her nipples adoringly. And Ella let his cock push into her just a little. *Oh my God.* It lit a fire to her arousal and her need to have him inside her was irresistible. Letting her body fall, she took him into her pussy in one fast motion and screamed out in pleasure.

Her heavy panting matched Adam's, and she fucked him hard. Rocking his hips up and down, Adam kept the same rhythm, gradually increasing to keep pace with her. Ella gave up all resistance. Throwing herself into the amazing feel of Adam stretching her wide, his heat burning inside her, she continued to pump his cock.

Nothing existed but Adam, his powerful maleness, and intense sexuality. Thrusting up and down, Ella took him as deep as he would go, but never let him free. Faster and faster they fucked, and she heard her own shrill whimpers as if they came from elsewhere. Looking into Adam's eyes, she saw a blaze of lust, and her clit burned.

Without warning, a heavy, sensual feeling swamped her and her clit turned so hard it hurt. She convulsed around Adam's hot cock. Over and over, Ella pulsed, strong and deep. She felt his cock surge and then he was coming once again, *with her* this time. Her orgasm went on and on, so long she thought it might never end.

And even when it did, Ella still felt a lasting ecstasy, a soul-wrenching passion that would never diminish. Never be muted. Never ripped away. No matter what happened, she would feel the deep desire she felt for Adam. And the all-consuming love. Nothing could take that away. Ever.

Chapter 8

Through the weekend and into the following week, nothing alarming happened. Ella felt calmer but she didn't let her guard down. And Adam met with Nico to coordinate their strategy. With family and friends arriving from California, and a long list of wedding attendees, security was strengthened. All guests would be staying at the Copacabana Palace Hotel, a reputable establishment with its own protection for guests.

At the church or during any sightseeing outings, it would be up to Nico to run the team. If he needed more help, he was to hire it, though he'd already added to the ranks. Adam's top priority was the safety of his family, and knowing that Claudio did not have equal resources did not persuade him to relax the safe perimeter around those he loved.

He tried to stay positive, but remained alert to anything out of the ordinary. Yet one day followed the next, and nothing unusual happened. On Wednesday of that week, Ella's mother, Jeanne, flew safely into Rio, and was transported to the hotel. Not long after, Julianna arrived from San Diego. And later in the afternoon, Kaiyla and Steve made their appearance.

Leaving nothing to chance, Adam sent private limos staffed with his own hired guards to pick them up at the airport as they came in. All vehicles were bullet proof, as most public transportation vehicles were in the city. There was no mishap, and once everyone got settled in their respective rooms, Adam and Ella went over to greet them.

Jeanne was resting from the long trip, and Julianna wanted to shower before the evening meal to freshen up after the long flight. Kaiyla and Steve were a bit jet-lagged but had no intention of spending time in their room when they could enjoy Rio. Neither had ever been to Brazil, and their excitement showed.

Adam and Ella met them at the poolside bar on the ground floor. Though Kaiyla was travel weary, her peppy personality never sagged. With her blond hair tied up in a loose ponytail and her green eyes bright, if helped by extra makeup, she looked ready for anything. Dragging Steve by the hand, she bounced over to the table and grabbed Ella for a hug.

"We made it."

"Yes, you sure did. You're actually in Rio." Ella hugged her too, and was very glad to see her. Everything was going to be so much better with her friend there to share it.

Steve took Kaiyla's place and embraced Ella. "Good to see you." Then he shook hands with Adam.

Ella chatted away with Kaiyla about the details of the wedding, while Adam and Steve found guy things to talk about. One of the most exciting days of Ella's life was coming up, and she wanted to include her friend in everything. Being Kaiyla, she listened with avid interest, interjecting questions and making comments, until Ella felt like they were up to date with each other.

They each had a beer, and then another. It was a trendy bar, full of tourists. Ella could recognize them by their obvious awe of the environment. And the windows of the bar looked out to the pool and the bay just beyond. In the distance, the city and the mountains completed the scene. And late April was the perfect time to visit Rio, due to the warm, pleasant spring weather. Although there was really no bad time to visit, since temperatures in the city didn't vary widely year round.

Finally, Kaiyla's energy level seemed to sag, which prompted her to beg for a short nap before meeting for dinner.

"So, what's planned for tomorrow?" Kaiyla's bright enthusiasm contrasted with her jet-lagged body.

"Wait until you see. Adam and I are taking you sightseeing. It's amazing here. You're going to love it."

After hugging her friend again, Kaiyla started to make her way back to the elevator. Steve stayed by her side, holding her hand. "Okay," she called back. "See you in a bit. I'll be starving so don't be late."

Ella laughed. She'd forgotten how carefree life could seem around her friend. "No way we're missing dinner. Don't *you two* be late."

*****

Dinner was in one of the hotel restaurants, which the family was thrilled with. And it suited Adam, as they didn't have to leave the establishment. Any time they ventured out there would be greater risk. The famous hotel, located on the beach, had welcomed the rich and famous since the 1920s. It was a glamorous icon with a reputation for exemplary service, superb cuisine, and opulent luxury.

Ever since Fred Astaire and Ginger Rogers danced together at the Copacabana Palace in the movie *Flying Down to Rio*, the hotel had been the place to stay when visiting. Kaiyla was especially tickled with the history of the place, and even Ella's mother seemed to warm to it.

Each room was designed with fine period furniture and original works of art, giving it an elegant yet relaxed ambience. Breathtaking views were of the world-famous Copacabana beach or the city. It overwhelmed Julianna at first, reminding Ella that her sister had never traveled outside of California. Arriving in Rio must have seemed like an amazing dream. That was how it had seemed to

Ella the first time, too.

The service was fast and courteous. Plus the food was delicious. The restaurant was used to catering to tourists from around the world, and though the meals had a decidedly Brazilian touch, they were palatable for the most discriminating tastes. As they worked their way through various courses and sipped their drinks, everyone got to know each other a bit better.

Jeanne was quite friendly to Adam, which Ella was relieved to see. And the relationship between Adam and her sister seemed to flower in the relaxed atmosphere, away from life's normal pressures. It was the best time that Ella had ever had with her family, and she was encouraged by it.

After dessert, they went out to the terrace to enjoy the view. The warm night air allowed them to stay out longer than they might have. At one point, Ella noticed how tired her mother looked, and she suggested they go in. Jeanne seemed relieved and didn't argue about going on up to her room to rest for the hours of sightseeing the next day.

Julianna stayed a bit longer, chatting with Kaiyla about what she was going to wear to the wedding. They found more to talk about, covering travel, career, and even art preferences. That was the thing about Kaiyla: she made friends easily. And Ella's sister was no exception. They had known each other while growing up, but since Julianna was the younger sister she never got much attention. Now she was a peer, and they really hit it off.

When the evening was over, Adam guided Ella to the limo and the others found their way back to their rooms. The social interaction had drained Ella for no reason she could name. Hanging around with Adam's family was always so warm and relaxed. She guessed there was a certain level of stress dealing with her own. Though she was pleased that it had gone so well. It was a great start.

*****

The next morning, Adam and Ella didn't arrive too early,

wanting to let the family get some rest and have breakfast at the hotel. They'd even had time to walk down to the beach if they'd wanted to, and may or may not have been aware of the guards assigned to them. They possibly just considered it part of being in Rio.

No one mentioned anything, and still early in the day, everyone piled into the rented Caravan. There was room for all six of them, plus Nico, who rode in the very back seat. He was introduced as their personal bodyguard, which did raise some eyebrows.

Ella just shrugged. "It's Rio."

Her casual attitude relaxed the others and revealed nothing of the concern she disguised. It would do no good to have them worry. Everything that could be done for their protection was being done. As for Ella, that was a different matter, because she knew Claudio's threat was directed specifically toward her.

Still, endless anxiety over it would not prevent anything. So she decided to enjoy the day and put anything else out of her mind. There was no question that Adam was concerned enough for the both of them and that Nico was on high alert. But none of that affected their activities in Rio that day.

Everything went well. And Ella even got to see some places she'd never seen before. First, they drove to Ipanema, made famous by the bossa nova song "The Girl from Ipanema." The two-mile-long stretch of white sand along the clear sky-blue water was packed with both tourists and Brazilians.

Against the backdrop of the gorgeous mountains, the locals played *futvolei,* or *footvolley* in English, which was beach volleyball but the players were not allowed to use their hands and a football was used instead of a volleyball. Really, it was a close relation to soccer.

The smell of fresh shrimp grilling nearby, and small bands stationed along the shoreline, added to the atmosphere. The beach had it all: great music, excellent food, sports, and beautiful people lazing in the sun. And if anything had been forgotten, vendors came to the rescue with towels, hats, beverages, snacks, jewelry, sunglasses, and beach chairs.

If Ella had brought her surfboard, she could have stayed all day. But she wasn't there solely for her own enjoyment. She walked the beach with everyone, listening to them chat, and realized how excited they were to be in Rio de Janeiro. Adam seemed a bit preoccupied, and she couldn't blame him.

The late-April wedding was just days away, and the burden of protecting everyone rested with him. He had Nico and a trained team, but if anything were to happen he'd never forgive himself. Ella intended to play her part to ensure nothing did. Though she wasn't sure what else she could do.

While the others gawked at the blue ocean, the high mountains, and the festive activity on the beach, Ella remained aware of what was around her. A second vehicle with more security had followed them to the beach, so she wasn't surprised to see strong men watching them attentively.

Kaiyla was in high spirits, and she wrestled free of Steve's hand to catch up to Ella.

Half laughing, she said, "Did you know Ipanema has a long tradition of dictating beach chic to the rest of the world?"

Ella giggled. "Oh, you don't say? I think you've been reading the brochures in your hotel room."

"I have. And you know what else?"

"I can hardly wait."

"This beach, the very one we are walking on, was a launching pad for the skimpy tanga bikini, the once-popular crocheted G-string for men."

Ella shoved her friend playfully. "Now that's something I really needed to know."

"There's more."

"I can hardly wait."

"It was also the birthplace of the unforgettable dental-floss bikini for women."

"I'm glad you are studying up on Brazilian history."

They both laughed.

"What are you girls laughing about?" Steve called out.

"Nothing," they said in unison.

Before leaving, they grabbed some grilled shrimp and coconut water at the beach. Then everyone piled into the van to head back to town. The next stop on the itinerary was one of the most beautiful buildings in center city: Rio de Janeiro Theatre.

Now they had Julianna's attention. Her study of art in college and her career at a gallery there prepped her with some knowledge of the subject. Seeing one of the most beautiful and important theaters in South America captivated her. The amazing architecture was a sight to behold. The exterior façade featured a stone staircase and marble columns several stories high placed between huge stained-glass windows.

"Ella, this place is stunning," Julianna remarked.

"Wait until you see inside." Ella waved everyone forward. "I've never been in but I've seen pictures."

Adam piped in, now paying more attention to his small group. "We'll be taking the tour so you will get to look all around."

Julianna pouted. "What if I don't understand what they are saying?"

Adam smiled. "Oh, you will. The tour guide gives the presentation in English...for all the tourists, you know."

"Well, let's go." Ella's mother had been reserved on the outing, but the luxurious façade of the culturally important building had sparked her interest.

Julianna put her hand on her mother's back to guide her inside.

Ella turned to Kaiyla. "So, did you study up on this too?"

Kaiyla grinned. "Yes, I sure did. Are you aware that Rio was once known as the 'Paris of Latin America'? Then all the beautiful old architecture was bulldozed to build more skyscrapers. But this building still stands, and has since been renovated. It's one of the gems that survived."

Steve put his arm around Kaiyla and gave her a hug. "She's a regular historian."

Ella laughed. "It would seem."

Adam looked back. "Are you ladies going to stay out here and talk, or are you coming in?"

"Coming in," Kaiyla called, and walked faster.

Once inside, they all stopped in awe of the main staircase that split into two, going sideways. Each was made of onyx, bronze, and gold. While they gawked, the Brazilian guide picked them up and began his narration.

"In the foyer, you see two masterpieces that stand out: the three stained-glass windows and the painted dome. The magnificent ceilings are in ceramic and the floors are Venetian mosaic."

He guided them to the concert hall and continued.

"The great central chandelier you see above is in gilded bronze. The restoration of this theater required thousands of sheets of twenty-three-carat gold from Germany."

Looking around, Ella saw gold everywhere, and she gazed up at the enormous chandelier. Just being inside the historical theater was like traveling back in time.

Next was the basement restaurant named Assyrio, unique with its impressive Assyrian décor. "Unique in all of South America," the guide said, "because the walls are covered with glazed pottery inspired by the ancient Babylon. And the mirrors are embedded in antique bronze."

Ella had stopped listening at some point. It was not that she wasn't interested; it was that the concern over what was to come refused to be kept at bay. For much of the time walking on the beach, or chatting, she had been able to put it out of her mind. But winding through the inside of the ancient building—which was awe inspiring but a bit ominous—brought back some of her trepidation.

She needed to get outside; that was all. Back in the sun and the fresh air. For some reason, she felt trapped, though she knew it wasn't because of the building. When the tour was over and they worked their way back to the street, Ella began to feel better. That was until she saw him.

Ella didn't say anything at first. Nico was close enough, but keeping some distance so as not to intrude on their family time. She'd begun to recognize the others he'd brought with him, and their presence made her feel safer. But then, standing at a distance near the corner of the theater, was an ugly man.

Why was he ugly? Probably it was his scowl, or the rumpled clothes he wore. She couldn't say. It was no one she recognized. And the area was thick with tourists. It could have been anyone. But he looked at her a little too long, and it attracted her attention. For a moment, she wasn't sure what to do.

Then she turned to catch Nico's attention, and he strode over to her immediately.

Ella let the others continue walking. Only Adam turned to follow her, noting her hasty retreat. He was beside her with his arm around her when she spoke.

Nodding toward the corner of the building, Ella said, "That man...over there...he—"

The man was gone.

Had she imagined danger where there was none?

"Who, Ella?" Nico looked around as he spoke.

"He's gone."

"Did you see someone, amore mia?"

"I thought so. Now I'm not sure. There are so many tourists. I might have imagined it. But he looked at me, like he had a reason to. You know, it was different."

Nico was already speaking into his earpiece, and two bodyguards made their way to the end of the building. Somehow Ella knew they wouldn't find anything. Nevertheless, she described him as best she could and then turned to go back to her family.

"They will be concerned. We better get back." Ella could already see the group facing them and starting to retrace their steps. It had been a good day until then. And Ella had hoped things would stay good, that nothing would happen. An idle threat, if only that was all it had been. But why fool herself? Claudio never gave up that easily.

Chapter 9

On the wedding day, the grooms were not allowed to see their brides in wedding gowns. But that didn't prevent the women from doing so. The dressing room was filled with an assortment of friends, all there to help. Fiorella had several assisting her into the lovely satin dress, and others ready to handle the last-minute primping to her hair and makeup.

Ella didn't have nearly so many, nor did she need them. Her mother and sister had already wished her well and were at the hotel getting dressed. Neither wanted to be in the wedding entourage, partly from shyness at the huge crowd that was expected and partly because they'd rather watch than perform. Both were relieved to hear that arrangements were taken care of and they should just enjoy the ceremony.

Ignoring any resistance from Steve about taking part in a formal wedding, Kaiyla readily accepted the invitation to participate. There were to be three couples on each side of the brides and grooms, and Fiorella easily filled those positions, including Kaiyla and Steve on Ella's side. Traditionally, the bridesmaids and groomsmen were picked as couples, not individuals.

Fussing over Ella's dress, her friend was attentive to every detail. She'd helped the hairdresser with styling, giving pointers on the finer details. After all, she was a beautician by profession. Never completely at ease in makeup, Ella didn't want anyone but her friend to do hers. It was a special day, and Kaiyla knew her preferences and was used to her skin tone.

The noise level grew as the time passed. Getting ready for a church wedding was no quick task. All the legalities had been taken care of and the preparations were done. Somehow the most nerve-racking was the getting-dressed part, at least for Ella. Most at home in a swimsuit on her surfboard, she still found formal settings awkward.

"You look beautiful!"

Kaiyla's admiration inspired confidence, and Ella looked in the mirror. She hardly recognized herself. With her long hair twisted up and clipped with rhinestone combs, and her makeup like something out of *Vogue*, she had to admit that she looked more amazing that she expected. And the dress was perfect. Not too much or too frilly, but lovely. And it subtly accented her slight curves.

Fiorella made her way across the crowded space with several women following her. She stopped in front of Ella.

"*Perfetto*! You look like a fairytale princess."

Ella understood the Italian word for "perfect." She never knew what language Fiorella might drift into. It seemed that depending on the emotion of the moment, it could be Italian, Portuguese, or English.

"So do you, Fiorella." And it was true. Ella looked at her future sister-in-law and grinned. "I love your hair that way, with the little white flowers in it."

"It took a lot of work. We've been doing this for hours." But she giggled. Fiorella didn't even look flustered.

And that was one of the things Ella loved about Brazil. Even the most important occasions never became stressful. It was all about family, friends, and celebrations. The whole noisy, crowded, bustling affair was just a big party from start to finish. And Ella was completely into the spirit of it.

"The *noivado* is about to be over." Fiorella continued to

beam at Ella.

"What?" Kaiyla was following the interaction between the two brides.

"She means the engagement." Ella grinned at her friend.

"Yes. Next...*casamento*." Fiorella looked very pleased indeed about that circumstance.

"Marriage," Ella said to Kaiyla, before she had a chance to ask what the word meant.

"Okay, well, this language lesson is loads of fun, but I have to go and find Steve. He will be totally lost. I'll see you out there." Kaiyla kissed Ella on the cheek and whisked out of the room.

Fiorella turned in front of the mirror and fluffed out the bottom of her dress. "You know Mamma is thrilled that we are getting married, all together, here in Metropolitan Cathedral. She's attended this church since she was a small girl, and it means a lot to her."

"I am honored. And I just want to say once again that I'm grateful that you could get us on the calendar."

"It wasn't easy, I'll tell you. Normally, weddings have to be scheduled a year in advance—at least."

"I think Serena pulled some strings."

Fiorella winked. "I know she did."

*****

The orchestra began to play "Ave Maria," and both grooms looked expectantly for their brides. The crowded pews were in a semi-circle, ever widening, around the pulpit where the Catholic priest stood. The walls around them were slanted, in keeping with the cone shape of the building, and the rectangular stained glass embedded from floor to ceiling shone a rainbow of colors over the assembly.

Adam was astounded by the ethereal feel, and his heart pounded in anticipation. He could see Adrian was every bit as excited. The music played loudly, and the entire crowd stood, as was the wedding tradition in Brazil.

69

Yellow and white flowers were everywhere. The friends and family there to share the important day were dressed in an array of colors.

In Rio, everyone wore their best to a wedding, though it was quite an assortment. Even the wedding party wasn't expected to be in perfect color harmony, since it was difficult to obtain matching dresses or tuxedos in the city. But that didn't matter. It was the spirit of the occasion that was everything, and Brazilians knew what that was about.

Serena sat in a place of honor in the front row. Adam could see she was already crying and dabbing at her eyes with a tissue. This was a big day for her, too, as both her children were getting married. He was grateful for her love and support; it made it better having her there. Among the sea of faces, Adam spotted some that he knew, but many he didn't.

It seemed no relative was too distant, or friend too casual, to invite to the wedding. Not if Fiorella was in charge of the planning. His heart warmed as he thought of his sister, and he was overjoyed that she would bind the union with Adrian, his longtime friend and her childhood sweetheart. She deserved the happiness she would find with her true love.

The flower girls entered first, dressed in frilly, colorful dresses and freshly polished shoes. Their hair was tied up in matching ribbons and they carried a basket from which they tossed flower petals as they walked forward. One would serve as the ring bearer, since the engraved gold wedding bands had been removed, only to be restored after the sealing of the vows. And this time placed on the left ring finger.

Behind the flower girls were the brides. Adam's breath caught when Ella entered. She was radiant in her stunning white dress, the rhinestones shimmering in the filtered light of the church. Her brown hair, piled high, sparkled from similar stones sprinkled through her sweeping curls. With each step, the tip of a gold shoe could be seen, and she carried a bouquet of yellow flowers, looking like an angel about to be received.

Though Adam could barely take his eyes from her, Fiorella attracted his attention. He'd never seen her look quite like she did. Maybe it was the glow she had, or the flowers in her hair. But he thought it was more her inner radiance. A beauty with her pale green eyes and reddish-brown hair, his sister was a delicate flower. Adam was aware of her adoring fiancé watching intently—the strength of their love was clear.

The brides glided down the aisle, one measured step at a time, followed by the numerous bridesmaids in pretty dresses and the groomsmen, each wearing a small Brazilian flag on their tuxedo lapel instead of a flower. They were all friends, and he was pleased to see Kaiyla and Steve included among them. A friendly face would mean so much to Ella at one of the most important moments in her life.

Photographers stationed along the way snapped pictures of the procession. Adam rolled his shoulders to relax, and unnecessarily adjusted his jacket. All arrived, and the grooms settled lovingly next to their brides, with the other attendants taking their place to the side. The young flower girls waited patiently, shifting a bit from one foot to the other, unable to contain their energy. Ella clung to Adam, and he could feel her trembling. He squeezed her hand, loving her with all his heart.

With everyone in place at the altar, the guests sat again on the wooden pews. A hush settled over the scene. Adam knew a typical Catholic wedding in some countries was very long, and likely boring. But the double wedding went fast. The priest didn't mess around with a sermon; he just got to the point, delivering his inspiring message forthwith.

A prayer was read in Portuguese. The words were unfamiliar to Ella. But she'd rehearsed plenty, and Adam knew that she had the whole thing nearly memorized. The couples stated their vows, and Ella said hers in English for the benefit of her mother and friends. The locals were not in doubt about what she was saying.

When Adam heard him say "*aliancas,*" asking the flower girl for the rings, he knew they were close. Ella's eyes went to the flower girl. The rings were placed on the brides' ring fingers, and at the appropriate point, the grooms slid them all the way on. And the brides returned the honor. Camera flashes sparked repeatedly, the photographers going crazy.

The priest pronounced to each couple that, with the blessings of God, they were now husband and wife, and followed with, "*Você pode beijar a noiva.*"

You may now kiss the bride. Adam put one hand at the base of Ella's neck and the other on her back, holding her tenderly, and she wrapped her arms around his neck. He'd kissed her before, but never like that. Not as husband and wife. The kiss went on so long that he only stopped when he heard the crowd screaming and shouting.

Reluctantly leaving his wife's lips, Adam stood and held her hand, raising it with the sweet bouquet high in the air. The cheering and clapping got louder. Fiorella and Adrian were hugging and laughing. And Ella was jubilant. Seeing her cheeks flushed and her brilliant smile, Adam's heart swelled with emotion.

As was common in Brazil, the witnesses signed the register to legitimize the service in front of the congregation, with no need to go behind closed doors. Photographers captured the ritual with more pictures. The solemn church bubbled with a festive roar now that it was all official.

Adam was so thrilled that he hugged his bride, lifted her off her feet, and swirled her around, wedding dress and all. Ella giggled and laughed. Letting her drift back to the floor, he released her to Kaiyla, who smothered her with kisses.

"Congratulations!" she kept saying in between kisses.

Steve wisely stayed out of the fray, but nodded at Adam in approval. When given a chance, he congratulated Ella, taking her hand and kissing her on the cheek.

Behind him, Fiorella pushed forward with Adrian by the hand, and motioned toward the exit, though escape wouldn't be quick. The rowdy crowd was harmless enough but not so easy to navigate through. Adam took Ella's hand and guided her though the mob, who swarmed them with kisses along the way, following close behind Adrian and Fiorella.

They made it as far as the first pew when Serena flew into their arms, hugging them each in turn. Adam nestled her in the protective family circle and they proceeded to navigate down the aisle. Music played over the talking and shouting. No one was in a big hurry to leave, despite the fact that a reception of food, drink, and more celebration awaited them at the hotel banquet room.

Once in the lobby, Adam opened his arms to his sister. She gave him a big hug and he kissed her on each cheek and then the forehead. Ella and Adrian joined in, and hugs with congratulations were given all around. Serena looked on with a non-stop grin. And for the grand finale, Adam gave his mother a big hug, lifting her in the air, and she squealed with delight.

*****

The wedding was in the evening with the reception immediately after. Dinner would follow—eventually. Ella had told her family to eat something before the ceremony because the main meal would not be served until midnight, as was the custom. There would be drinks and appetizers, but just to be safe it would be better not to arrive hungry.

The reception was held in one of the banquet rooms at the Copacabana. It didn't take long for the party to get underway. Drinks of all types were served, including beer, wine, champagne, and cocktails. Traditional Brazilian food was offered, starting with finger food. Also, *casadinhos*, or "marry well" cookies, were served to go with the drinks. And a band played music throughout the evening, both old American favorites and popular Brazilian tunes. At one point, they even played the Brazilian national anthem.

Ella felt closer to Adam than she ever had, though she could barely get a moment alone. More pictures were taken of both brides with their grooms, and then with their families. Friends, both old and new, drifted over in waves to hug and congratulate. Ella spotted Kaiyla across the room in full party mode, drinking and dancing. The fact that most attendees spoke only Portuguese didn't put her off in the least.

Jeanne seemed to be having a good time as well. And Ella saw her dance with a handsome Brazilian more than once. It reminded her that her mother had been alone for longer than she could ever remember, and was due to have a man steal her heart. It would be quite something if she fell for a Brazilian. Not too surprising, though, since Latin men were so romantic. Ella could attest to that.

Julianna seemed to have latched on to another woman who spoke English, and she was deep in conversation when Ella saw her. Most likely they were discussing art, a subject her sister enjoyed above all others. Ella was glad she'd been able to attend the wedding and see Rio. Plus, they had restored their sister-to-sister relationship, which was a welcome relief.

Fiorella pulled Adrian onto the dance floor mercilessly. She loved to samba, and there was ample opportunity. Bride or not, she intended to dance her fill, and have as much fun as any of the guests. At one point, the music paused, and Fiorella waved for Adam and Ella to join them. The two newlywed couples danced the waltz, to everyone's delight.

Normally, guests would toss donations into a basket in the center of the room as wedding gifts for the couple to assist them to start their new life together. The invitations had informed everyone that all donations would go to a worthy cause: one of Gustavo Cardoso's reformation projects.

Ever since the former drug lord had helped Ella when she had requested his assistance in getting Claudio to back off, there had been a constant flow of money toward his humanitarian efforts. Both Adam and Ella gave as they could, so nothing would make them happier than to funnel any wedding donations into his capable hands. Adrian and Fiorella followed suit, feeling that they were already immensely fortunate, and taking greater joy in seeing the gifts go to those in need.

Eating, drinking, and chatting with guests in rotation should have been exhausting, but Ella didn't find it so. Her feet were getting tired, though, so when dinner was at last served she gladly sank into a chair beside Adam at a table with the family. Serena sat next to a lady from church, and to her right were Violetta and Vitto. The evening had been so busy that Ella hadn't had a chance to even say hello to them. Across the noisy table, she called out a greeting and lifted a hand to wave. Violetta smiled and waved back.

Fiorella sat to the other side of Adam with Adrian and his parents. Quinn Bauer was there with Tia, a dark-haired beauty who looked ravishing in her purple cocktail dress. Ella had never seen Quinn so relaxed and informal. Next to Ella, her friend Kaiyla pressed against her, with Steve holding her hand.

Leaning over, she said in Ella's ear, "This is so fun. You should get married every day."

Ella laughed. "You're next. I can't wait to come to your wedding."

"I'll have to come up with something pretty good to beat this."

A flood of waiters served the main course efficiently. It was feijoada, the national dish, a stew composed of slow-cooked meats, black beans, and spices. Actually, it was *feijoada completa*, the complete meal, which included fresh orange slices, rice with peppery onion sauce, chopped collard greens, and farinha, a yellowish root-vegetable flour.

She pressed her thigh against Adam's and watched him eat. With all the activity, and considering the lateness of the hour, Ella should have been hungry. But after a couple of delicious bites, she was done. There was just too much excitement, with more to come. Her stomach just couldn't settle down enough for her to enjoy the hearty food.

Instead, she sipped her champagne. Dinner was well received but the party showed no signs of slowing. Fiorella had told her to expect it to go until three or four in the morning. And so it did. While the music and dancing never stopped, the multilayered white wedding cake trimmed with ornate red roses was cut, and consumed, without anyone missing a beat.

The enthusiasm for dancing increased if anything, and more drinks were served, more food brought out. Ella didn't even feel the champagne, though she'd had many glasses of it, and figured she had burned it off with the samba dancing. Dancing had another advantage in that it was a way to be alone with Adam. If she could call it being alone, with the throngs of other dancers surrounding them.

When Adam looked at her, as only he could, no one else existed. As a new bride, she had eyes only for her handsome husband. Ella could hardly believe it had really happened. She remembered mailing the gold-embossed invitations: *Ella Walker and Adam Bianci request the honor of your presence...*

It had sounded like a dream. And now it had happened. She was his wife, and she knew she wasn't going to come down from the clouds for a long time, if ever. Finally, Adam put his arms around her, and whispered in her ear, "Let's get out of here, amore mia. I still have plans for you on your wedding night."

"And *I* have plans for *you*," she whispered back. And off they went to say goodbye for the evening, well past three in the morning, while the party showed no signs of losing momentum.

Chapter 10

In the back of the limo, Ella leaned her head on Adam's shoulder. It had been an amazing day of excitement and activity, and tiredness seeped into her now that she had a moment of quiet. She could easily claim exhaustion, but there was no way she'd fall asleep on her wedding night. Not with her husband's firm body so near.

Ella yawned but stifled it. "I guess everybody will be okay without us." If anything were to happen, it wouldn't have been at the church. Even the worst criminals didn't perpetrate their deeds within the holy walls. And the hotel was protected by no less than a small army, with Adam's team plus the hotel's own security.

Adam placed his hand on her thigh and played with the white satin fabric, his touch sensual and promising. "You can be sure they will be well cared for." He touched her cheek, his tone shifting. "I'm impatient to have you alone."

The way he said it in a piercing, demanding tone was hot.

Snuggling her head against his shoulder, Ella said, "I'm so glad we will have a few days alone."

Adam replied, his deep voice laced with emotion, "Away from the family, tucked away, *just you and I.*"

Hotel Santa Teresa was only fifteen minutes from Copacabana, but the distance didn't need to be hundreds of miles to isolate the new couple from the barrage of well-wishing family and friends. The newlyweds had gone away together, and no one would bother them. Later in the year they planned for a longer honeymoon, when the surfing was better, but right then a couple of days with no one else around sounded wonderful.

The wood floors, rough earth-toned plaster walls, and dark furniture were reminiscent of the Brazilian tropics, and Ella felt like she was hidden away in the depths of Rio. Once inside, she removed her high heels, feeling the cool surface against her sore feet. Adam removed his black jacket and tie, and undid the top buttons of his shirt. Next came the cufflinks, then the shoes and socks.

"There, that's better." He reached into a leather case and retrieved his iPod, setting it in the dock in the music system. Flipping it on, he started music playing—one of Ella's favorite Luciana Souza songs, "Here It Is." The intimacy of the Brazilian singer's distinctive voice filled the room, and when Adam reached for Ella she fell into his arms.

In an easy embrace, Adam began to guide her in dance, slowly, sensually moving to the intensely romantic harmony. The notes echoed against the wooden floor beneath their feet and reverberated against the stucco walls. His strong body wrapped around her, guiding her in a pattern around the room. Warmth spread through her body and settled in her core.

If she'd ever wanted Adam, she wanted him then. But finally alone, he seemed to have every intention of making the evening last. It was her wedding night, one she'd always remember, and with her swoon-worthy husband so close, time lost all meaning. They danced to that song, and the next, pressed together in agonized longing. Cherishing every second.

In a relaxed, dreamy posture, Adam released her and went to open a bottle of champagne that had been left chilling in a bucket of ice. He popped the cork and filled two glasses, then handed one to her.

Lifting the glass toward hers, Adam toasted. "To my beautiful wife."

Ella lifted hers. "To my sexy husband."

The lust in Adam's eyes was evident, and she suspected he was using every shred of self-control not to rip the wedding dress off of her and consummate the marriage. But that wasn't his nature. Every time they were together, it was never hurried and always special. Now, in the early hours before dawn, Adam sipped his champagne, watching Ella drink hers.

He looked so sexy with his golden tan, his hair mussed, and his shirt partly open. Seeing him take another sip, Ella couldn't look away from his mouth. The way he placed the glass, just so, letting the bubbly liquid roll over his tongue and down his throat. Even when he swallowed, it turned her on. Without touching her or saying a word, he was driving her crazy with desire.

Adam put his glass on the table and reached for Ella's to do the same. With him standing so close, she could feel his breath on her skin, and the electricity between them was palpable. She put her hands on his chest, feeling the hard muscle beneath the white fabric. Inpatient, she undid the buttons with shaky fingers and pulled the shirt off, revealing more of Adam's sculpted form.

Running her hands over his golden skin and fingering the soft hair covering his chest, Ella felt weak. He placed his palms on her cheeks and tipped her face toward his. The kiss he gave was warm and loving, with something more simmering under the surface. His lips were soft, and he tasted of the champagne and a potent male flavor that was uniquely Adam's.

The kiss became harder, more insistent, and he pressed his body to hers with no need to hide his desire. He was hard under the formal pants he still wore, and knowing that made Ella a little dizzy. God, she wanted him. She always wanted him. The feeling was all consuming. Reaching behind, he placed his hands over her bottom and pressed her closer.

When he pulled back from the kiss, Ella gasped for breath. "Adam...Adam."

His eyes glistened with need. "I want you to do something for me, amore mia. All evening, watching you float among the guests, seeing you move, watching you walk, turned me on more than I can say. Then dancing...dancing with you. The way you step, kick your legs, sway your hips...it drove me insane. And all the while, do you know what I was thinking?"

Ella looked on, waiting.

"Of you, beautiful one, and how you looked under the innocent satin dress. Of your flawless bronzed skin under the virgin white of your gown."

Ella swallowed thickly, her mouth dry.

"But even more. I fantasized all evening, hour after tortuous hour, about pulling down your tiny satin panties and seeing your firm, round ass naked below the formal dress."

Ella felt weak.

"And I want to see you now. I want you to lift this frilly dress that disguises your truly erotic nature. I need to see you naked. Please turn around for me, sweet Ella, and grasp the back of that chair."

With her clit so hard she could barely move, Ella turned and did as he'd asked. Gripping the wood of the chair, she bent over. With purposeful movements, Adam lifted the long white skirt of her wedding gown and piled it above her hips onto her low back. She could feel the ambient air waft over her skin.

For Adam, she'd worn a satin garter belt and real silk white stockings, knowing he would undress her on their wedding night. Right then, she knew he was admiring that view; the only other thing covering her was a thin satin thong. She felt his hot fingers when he reached under the elastic of the thong and pulled it slowly down to her ankles.

Her ass was bare, and he took his time drinking in the sight. It felt so erotic, standing there bent over, still in the expensive wedding dress, her hair still up, glittering with rhinestones. But with her bare ass open to view, open for *Adam* to view. It was decadent, sexy. Her legs trembled and anticipation escalated.

He placed his hands on her bare skin, nearly scorching her with his heat, and he squeezed. It was a deliriously sensual touch and sent heavy warmth deep into her core. Ella panted softly, willing for Adam to do anything he wanted. She would deny him nothing and would give him everything.

Holding the tops of her thighs, Adam kissed her buttocks with hot, needy kisses, making her so wet it began to seep down her leg. *Jesus.* Raking his tongue over her sensitive skin, he drove her higher into a potent ecstasy. Every nerve in her body was alert, responding to every caress. He gripped her ass, spreading her cheeks slightly, and licked between.

No one had ever done that to her before, and she'd never known it could be so sexy. Adam gently massaged her naked ass, relentlessly pushing her toward a release she tried to forestall. Then he pressed his thumb against her tight asshole. It was surprising but felt deliciously good. Its taboo nature added to the excitement.

With Adam, she could do anything. With Adam, she *would* do anything. But there was one thing Ella wanted then, more than any other thing. And that was his thick cock buried inside her. Almost as if he read her mind, he stood and leaned over her, placing his hands next to hers on the back of the chair. He kissed her neck with urgency.

Ella whimpered and thought to beg, but knew that she didn't need to. Adam reached back and undid his pants, pulling them down along with his shorts, so she could feel his erection against her. Molten heat ran through her lower body and flooded her sex. She pressed back against him.

He cupped her sex then played over her clit. Whimpering louder and panting faster, Ella tried to cope. With his other hand, Adam squeezed her breasts, and even under the elaborate material Ella could feel the exquisite pressure, and her already distended nipples ached in response.

Then she felt Adam's swollen cock between her legs, and it was insanely sexual. She would have said something, cried out in pleasure, if she could have spoken at all. He began rocking his hips so that the top of his length stroked along her sopping slit. Ella thought she might come on the spot, but she didn't want to. She never wanted it to end; was never able to get enough.

Bent over as she was, Ella's pussy was fully accessible. When Adam slid his hard knob past her outer lips and into her softer interior, she gasped. *Oh God.* Instinctively, she pushed her hips toward him, taking more of him. Gradually, his cock slid deeper, stretching her.

With her pussy around him, Adam stroked with precise back-and-forth motions of his hips. Ella closed her eyes and gripped the chair tighter.

"I love you naked," he said in a gasping moan. "I...I crave you."

The ability to restrain sensation vanished in that second. Ella lost all sense of reality. There was only Adam. Only his cock buried as deep as it would go. Only the intense feeling that burned through her sex and stiffened her clit to the point of pain. Only that and nothing more.

Faster and faster, Adam fucked her, rocking them back and forth, the chair shuddering under the pressure. Then his thick cock pulsed hard and Ella let go. Powerful waves took hold of her and she screamed with abandon, while Adam pulsed repeatedly inside her and groaned like a virile animal caught in a trap of unendurable pleasure that bordered on pain.

Together they came, husband and wife, lovers out of control. The pleasure lasted and lasted, sensation flooding Ella's body mercilessly, and even when her pussy stopped pulsing, the waves of release did not, just gradually lessened. But the amazing feeling didn't go. When Adam pulled out of her and turned her to face him, Ella still felt orgasmic. She'd never felt anything like it.

Holding her close, Adam let her skirt fall back to the floor, and he stroked her hair lovingly. Her pulse still pounded and she could feel his heart beating hard in his chest. Ella wrapped her arms around his waist and clung to him, vulnerable. The love she felt merged them into one. There was no separation, just them, alone together.

Pale gray light began to appear, brightening the windows and announcing dawn was near. But Ella had no intention of sleeping. Not yet. She kissed Adam's chest then his neck. He turned her around to unzip the tantalizing wedding dress and helped her out of it. Then he adoringly unclipped her stockings and removed them. He undid her bra and cast it aside, leaving her in nothing but a diamond necklace.

He was already fully undressed, and she teased him with a fake pout.

"I didn't get to undress you."

Adam smiled, his eyes sparkling. "The tuxedo?"

"Yes, the tuxedo, which is so sexy on you."

"Hmm, I'll have to remember that."

"God had you in mind when he created tuxedos."

"I didn't know a black tux was heavenly garb."

"It is when you wear it."

Adam scooped her into his arms and headed toward the bedroom. "I'll get an entire wardrobe of tuxedos, then. Anything for my beautiful wife."

Chapter 11

The next day was Sunday, and the couple, madly in love and exhausted by the time the sun blazed through the windows, slept late. Very late. In fact, they were in the hotel restaurant to eat at two in the afternoon, showered, refreshed, and ready to enjoy every minute they had together. They sat on the terrace of the restaurant looking out at Santa Teresa, sprawled at the top of a hill, and offering a magnificent view of Guanabara Bay.

It was too late for breakfast, but the lunch menu offered many options. They shared pan-fried salmon with chipotle pepper and salad, accompanied by grapefruit and cassava fries. Washing it down with lime-flavored mineral water, they leaned back to take a break while waiting for their espressos to arrive.

Adam held his new wife's hand and looked at the gold band on her left finger. "I love you so much, Ella."

Under the table, she rubbed her ankles next to his. "I love you with all my heart, Adam. I'll always love you. Always."

The steaming espressos arrived and they began sipping the rich Brazilian coffee.

Ella put her tiny china cup back on the matching saucer. "I'm glad we got to say goodbye to Fiorella and

Adrian before we left last night."

"Yes, and I told her not to even think about Fiore's while they are away. She's hired competent staff to oversee the day-to-day operations, and I assured her for the hundredth time that I'm here if anything is needed."

"Her restaurant means so much to her. I can understand how hard it is to get away. But she has been planning her honeymoon for years."

"Yes, Adrian has had enough time to save money for it. Since she was a young girl she has wanted to go to Argentina. It's not even that far, but still, somewhere you just never get to."

"And thankfully, Adrian was able to get a full three weeks away from the law firm. They will have a great time."

"No kidding. Weeks of food, wine, and countryside."

"Sounds like home."

Adam laughed. "It does. Well, they will be in Mendoza part of the time. I hear the local food there is remarkable. Maybe she will meet some Italians and learn a few Argentina-style Italian dishes."

"She told me there are lots of Italians in Argentina."

Adam took the last sip of his espresso. "Feel like getting out?"

"What...you think you're so irresistible that I'd spend all three days here locked in the hotel room with you?"

"Well, I am pretty irresistible."

Ella swatted his arm playfully. "Okay, show me the town, Romeo."

The town was filled with cultural centers, restaurants, and live music. Adam and Ella toured around on foot, making their way through the winding, narrow cobblestone streets. The area had resisted development and retained its colonial charm. When they tired of walking up and down, they took the streetcar. They saw everything from sidewalk mosaics and palatial mansions to artsy galleries.

Over their brief stay, they spent part of the afternoons

lounging on the terrace of their suite, enjoying the panoramic view. One day they went down to the poolside bar, drank beer, and talked for hours. Though they tried several restaurants in town, there was none better than the chef in the dining room at their hotel.

Originally from France, he'd later discovered Latin American tastes, so the cuisine combined the best French cuisine techniques with sophisticated Brazilian flavors. The codfish risotto with green chilies was Ella's favorite. Twice they went there for dessert, unable to resist the half-bitter chocolate mousse cake with passionfruit.

They even found time to surf. Ella was grateful that Adam had thought to bring their surfboards. And most of all, they made love whenever they felt like it, any time of day or night. Each interlude was intense, hot, and an expression of the craving they had for each other that could never be satisfied. On the morning they left to return home, Ella wished they'd planned for a longer stay.

The limo—with their trusted driver Miguel at the wheel—took them safely back to the beach house, with Nico and two other bodyguards following in another vehicle. They'd guarded them every hour of the day while the rest of the team had looked after the family. Fiorella and Adrian were already well into their honeymoon. And life drifted back toward normal.

Ella's mother and sister had already returned to California. She'd said her goodbyes at the reception. They'd been catered to in the last days of their visit. Adam had procured a tour guide for them, and along with a team of loyal bodyguards, they'd had a chance to see many of the other tourist draws in Rio.

At the beach house, Adam caught up with emails since he hadn't connected at all while they were gone, and Ella made a short entry in her diary. Sitting by the pool, relaxed in a lounge chair, she felt immensely happy.

I'm married, dear diary. It really happened. And if Adam was amazing before, he is even more so now. It

86

was a fairytale week. Everyone got along with each other, and Rio worked its magic. My mother even showed affection. And my sister seemed pleased again to be my sister. Of course, my other family was amazing, like they always are. Yes, Serena is now my mother-in-law. And Fiorella and Adrian are in-laws, too. I am really part of the family.

The best part is being Adam's wife. There are no words to express the joy he brings to me. I'm going to be the best wife ever. Maybe I'll even learn to cook more. But he doesn't seem to care either way. That's one thing about him. Adam doesn't make demands or try to change me. He loves me the way I am. And we just have fun together.

I haven't forgotten about his father. But nothing happened to disrupt the wedding. Except there was that one day when I thought I saw a man watching me. But I might have just been freaking out. Seeing that letter—and hearing that he might do something to me if Adam doesn't give him the money he asks for—was shocking.

I didn't let on because I know Adam worries enough. I have to be brave and stay strong. Maybe Claudio will ease up. Maybe there is money that will satisfy him. He is Adam's father, after all. If he'd just behave like it, all this wouldn't be happening. His son is one of the most generous men I've ever met. He wouldn't slight his own father if the man would just show some decency.

But no, he has to use threats of violence and pressure for money. He's a criminal, so I guess that's the only way he knows. We won't be bullied. And I refuse to kowtow to him. It's not right. I thought when he fled to Paraguay that it was the end of his harassment. But he didn't learn, it seems. Well, he won't win. He can't win.

*****

Early the next morning, before the limo took Steve and Kaiyla to the airport, Ella went to the hotel to say goodbye. Adam had a meeting with his sales manager, so sent his regards. It had been nice having her friend visiting, and Ella was sad for her to go. At least she'd see her when they went back to California, though they didn't know when that would be.

Kaiyla opened the door to her room. "Hey, Ella. How was the honeymoon getaway?"

Ella grinned. "Unbelievable. How long do you have?"

"We don't leave for a couple of hours. Steve is showering. Want to grab some coffee?"

"Yes, absolutely."

Kaiyla waved Ella inside and told her to wait a minute while she let Steve know she was going out for a bit. Then they took the elevator to the lobby. Rounding the corner, they spotted the café, but it wasn't open quite yet.

"Darn." Kaiyla threw her hair back over her shoulder, clearly needing the coffee they sought.

"Well, we can go somewhere else," Ella said. "How about that place just up the street?"

"Sure, they know how to make a good latte. Let's go."

Ella glanced around for Nico, since he was always nearby. Then remembered she'd left him on the other side of the lobby. He thought she was still upstairs with Kaiyla, and in any case he was used to waiting. It was part of his job. They were burning up valuable time. If they didn't settle on a coffee place, it would be time for her friend to leave for the airport.

"Okay, give me a sec. I'll let Adam know so he won't worry." Ella sent a text, though she knew he was in a meeting and might not even see the message.

"Let's catch one of the limos in front of the hotel. They're always lined up there."

"Good idea. We'll have you back upstairs in less than an hour."

The driver secured them in the back seat and made the short trip to the coffee shop. Kaiyla and Ella chatted away, then they hopped out at the local establishment, intending to chat more. Ella handed some money to the driver and asked him to wait for them.

"We won't be too long. She has to get to the airport."

The driver nodded and watched them hustle into the shop. They gulped their drinks while trading details of Ella's stay in Santa Teresa, and tales of the places Kaiyla and Steve had visited in Rio over the recent days. Minutes flew by, and before they knew it, it was time to leave.

"I hate for you to go. Promise you will come back again. I love having you in Rio."

Kaiyla laughed. "Well, I'd love to. And it was so generous of Adam to pay our expenses. But I doubt he plans to make that a habit."

"I'll twist his arm."

"You do that. Anyway, we'll see each other when you come home."

They looked at each other.

Ella grinned. "I am home."

"Good point." Kaiyla hugged her. "All right, wedding girl, get me back to the hotel before I miss my flight."

The driver opened the door for them. He'd removed his hat. Ella hadn't taken much notice of him before, but he did look different without the hat. She slid in next to Kaiyla and they made the short trip to the Copacabana.

"This is it. I have to go right up and make sure Steve finished packing."

Ella hugged her again. "Give him my love. I'll have the driver take me around to the lot. I texted Nico and told him to meet me there."

Kaiyla hopped out, and Ella waved. She really was going to miss her.

After her friend disappeared inside, the limo rolled forward along the front of the hotel, never accelerating. But it didn't turn into the driveway of the parking lot.

"There," Ella said. "Turn there." The driver did not respond or even look at her.

The car didn't stop, and Ella heard a *thunk* when the doors automatically locked. Panic hit her. What was going on?

"What are you doing? You're going the wrong way." She

pounded on the back of the driver's seat.

One block up, the limo pulled to the curb and the doors unlocked. Terrorized, Ella reached for the door handle to get out, and planned to give the driver a real chewing out. But another muscle-bound Hispanic male slipped in the back seat next to her. Reacting as quickly as she could, Ella reached for the other door handle.

It was too late. The door was already locked. Roughly the man grabbed her, and Ella screamed, knowing the vehicle was likely soundproofed and no one would be able to hear her. Then the man grabbed her arm in a meaty fist and stuck her with a needle. Ella felt the sharp prick when it penetrated her skin.

No! Desperation hit her like a brick wall. *Adam...help me.* The stench of the man suffocated her. Consciousness faded quickly like a heavy velvet curtain coming down, turning everything black.

Chapter 12

Adam leaned back against the chair in Quinn's office. He'd only been away for a few days but his attorney had a lot to go over with him. The week before the wedding had been hectic, and not much had gotten done then. After days alone with his bride, it was difficult to be separated from her. When his phone vibrated he looked down and quickly read her text.

Coffee with Kaiyla shouldn't take long, and if he could wrap up his meeting, then he'd see his new wife. The weather was perfect; maybe they would go surfing.

"Adam, did I lose you?" Quinn furrowed his brow.

Adam nodded. "Sorry, I got distracted."

"Text?"

"Yes, Ella is just seeing her friends off before they leave for the airport."

"Still in honeymoon mode, amico mio?"

Adam chuckled. "Guess so. Anyway, on what we were discussing, you are the operations manager for AB Software. I trust your judgment. Just go with it."

"Sure, we'll go over it more at a different time." Quinn rolled his shoulders to loosen the stiffness and then stood. "Coffee?"

"That would be good. As long as Ella is still visiting I may as well hang around."

"Great wedding reception, by the way."

"It was, wasn't it? Fiorella really packed the place. My sister loves a party. What time did it break up?"

"Well, Tia and I left just before four. It was slowing down then."

"Tia and you seem like an item. Is it serious?"

Quinn shrugged. "It might be. We will see."

Over coffee, the two friends talked about various things. It was a casual conversation. Adam had known his attorney for most of his life, and he was just as much friend as business associate. He'd done a lot to ensure stability for Adam's growing software company.

And with his dark hair, olive complexion, and good build, Quinn was admired by the ladies. But he was as loyal as he was friendly, and tended to stick with one woman rather than carouse around. His first marriage had ended badly, so Adam hoped things would work out with Tia, his girlfriend of several months now.

More than ever, Adam felt lucky. He'd found Ella and now she was his wife. He couldn't get over it. Finding the right woman had seemed out of reach for so long. Growing up, he was the computer nerd that women steered clear of. Being handsome didn't seem to compensate. Though he knew the women looked, they thought he was a bit of a brain, and kind of odd.

They were right. Adam hadn't been given the opportunity to perfect his social graces, always inside working out programming issues. His father had done his best to keep him working, for money-motivated reasons, and had no concern for his son's emotional development. But there had always been Serena to counter the effects of his father.

His mother had done her best to protect him, even when he was young. But she could only do so much. Fiorella could do little except love him, which she always had. She was a bright spot in his life, and would remain so. In adulthood, he still had a close relationship with her, and did what he could to ensure her happiness.

Then there was Ella. When Adam had first met her, it was clear she was special. It was the first time he'd connected so effortlessly with a woman. She understood him, and despite his unusual personality, didn't think he was weird. On the contrary—she loved him and had from the start. He had complete faith in his wife and would honor what they had with each other. Ella meant everything to him.

After wrapping up the meeting, Adam's driver took him home. He hoped Ella would already be there. Though they had only been apart for a couple of hours, he missed holding her and feeling her near. He looked forward to the real honeymoon they had planned; it couldn't come soon enough to suit him.

He saw Ella's tablet on the kitchen counter and smiled, knowing she still liked to write about him. But he had no need to pry; they had no secrets between them. Whatever thoughts she'd shared with her diary, she'd surely shared with him. And more.

Looking out at the surface of the pool, he recalled their recent honeymoon. The wedding night, once they were alone, had been unforgettable. Ella in her white wedding dress was burned in his mind, and his thoughts drifted to sexier memories. His loins stirred and he ran his hand through his hair.

Where was she?

His phone vibrated. It was Nico.

"Are you on your way back?"

"Not yet."

"Is Ella with you?"

"That's what I called to tell you. We arrived early and she went up to Kaiyla's room. Ella texted to confirm Kaiyla and Steve were there, so I waited in the lobby."

"So she's still up there?" Adam tried to do the math in his head. It didn't make sense that she'd still be with her friend. He seemed to recall their flight was mid-morning.

"No. I got a second text from her, about an hour and a half later. It said I should meet her in the lot."

"Why wouldn't she just meet you in the lobby?"

"It didn't say. So, I went to the lot, but I haven't seen her. I tried to text but I haven't gotten a reply."

Adrenaline flooded Adam's system. He worked to remain calm. So far, he didn't know for sure that anything was wrong.

Nico continued: "I checked with the desk and Kaiyla just left with Steve. I went back up to the room anyway, but it was empty."

Panic struck Adam. "What could have happened? Where could she be?"

"My next move would be to phone our limo driver. He's taking them to the airport. But I thought it best to check with you. I don't want to alarm them unnecessarily. However, at this point I recommend quick action. If something has happened, which I feel it has, I'd like to move on it."

"Yes, I agree. Let me call, and I'll get right back to you."

Adam quickly dialed the number Quinn gave him, and got the driver on the line.

"Are Kaiyla and Steve with you?" Adam prayed he would learn something from Kaiyla to resolve the sudden scare, and make everything right.

"Yes, sir."

Adam tried to sound normal. "Is everything all right?"

"Yes, sir. In fact, we left a little early so it should be no problem getting them to their flight on time." The driver sounded quite pleased with himself, misunderstanding the reason for Adam's call.

"That's excellent to hear. Take good care of them for me. Can you put Kaiyla on the line?"

Adam waited.

"Adam?"

"Good morning, Kaiyla."

Ella's friend sounded relaxed, showing no sign that anything bad had happened. "Oh, it's so good of you to call. I'm sorry we missed you this morning but I understand that you had a meeting. Steve and I both want to thank you again for your hospitality. You have no idea how much we appreciate being able to attend your wedding. And seeing Rio."

Adam barely heard what she said. "Sure, yes. No problem. Uh, and you got to see Ella this morning?"

"Yes, that was so nice of her. She came to say goodbye. We went out for coffee."

"Went out?"

"Sure, well, not Steve. He was showering. But Ella and I got time to say goodbye."

Adam held his breath. "Downstairs?"

Cheerfully, Kaiyla enlightened him. "No, they weren't open yet. But that place you took us to, just down the street, they open really early. We went there."

Adam's heart pounded.

"Kaiyla, how long were you there?"

"Not too long. Why? Haven't you talked to Ella?"

He didn't want to alarm her; it wouldn't help.

"Oh, I just got out of my meeting. I'll probably talk to her in a minute. So, you guys had time to walk over to the coffee shop?"

"We didn't bother with that. The limos are so convenient. We just took one of those."

Now, Adam feared the worst. "And walked back?"

"No, we didn't have to. Ella asked our driver to wait. Why do you ask?"

Why? What could Adam tell her?

"Oh, just checking on hotel amenities." Adam gave his best mock-casual laugh.

"You're funny. Well, give Ella a hug for me. I'll be in touch."

Adam's heart wrenched. His greatest desire was to give Ella a hug. But that wasn't looking too promising.

"Sure, Kaiyla. I'll do that. Did Ella walk you back up to your room, you know, to make sure you got there okay?"

"You are the protective one. No, she didn't need to. I just hopped out and she texted Nico to meet her in the parking lot. The limo was going to take her around. So she should be home soon."

"Great. That's great. Okay, have a good flight. Talk to you later."

Adam clicked off, feeling numb. Less than an hour before, Kaiyla had been with Ella. And Ella had been in a hotel limo. Then where was she?

Nico picked up instantly when he called back.

"I spoke to Kaiyla. Here's what we know: she went down the street for coffee. A hotel limo drove them, and waited for them. After dropping Kaiyla out front, the driver was supposed to take Ella to the lot where she texted you to meet her."

"I'm already checking with hotel services. They had three limos out front this morning. One hasn't returned. The driver reported that he was taking two female passengers about a block away and waiting for them. But that's the last report."

"Who was the driver?"

"I'm having them check the files. I'll get back to you."

Fearing the worst, Adam paced the room. Being at home while Ella was out there somewhere in danger, he felt helpless. Anger boiled inside. It wasn't right that he practically had to keep his wife locked in a fortress to keep her safe. He was going to get his hands on Claudio and handle this once and for all.

But how? He knew his father, and Adam tried to think like he would. It was still doubtful that Claudio had returned to Rio. It wasn't safe for him, and he wasn't brave by nature. As previously thought, he had an accomplice. Or more than one. Money could buy allies, at least temporarily. And they would only be needed until the ransom was handed over.

That had to be it. Ella had been taken as a guarantee that Adam would meet his father's demand. The move was brash, considering Claudio had resisted that temptation before. He'd told Ella he didn't want to be hunted by the American government for abducting one of their citizens. His father must be more desperate than ever, as now he

96

seemed to flaunt that powerful authority.

His phone vibrated. Irrationally, he hoped it was Ella. After looking at the caller ID, he answered, "Nico, what have you got?"

"I spoke with the limo driver myself."

"And?"

"He's new with the hotel, but they did a background check and he has a clean record. Came with good references. He had worked the early morning shift, and he would have been off soon. Says another driver came to relieve him."

"He turned the car over to a different driver?"

"Right."

"Did he know the guy?"

"No, but then he's new and doesn't know all the staff yet."

"Where is the driver that took over?"

"Gone. The car didn't return, nor did the driver. All other on-duty staff are accounted for and vehicles are where they should be. Whoever was driving that car, nobody knows him."

Adam was getting frustrated. "So he just impersonated a hotel limo driver and drove off with Ella?"

"It would seem so."

"Merda!" Adam rarely swore in Italian, but the situation made him furious. "Can that driver give a description?"

"Yes, but it could fit many people. You know, with the uniform and all, they look very much alike. He looked Brazilian."

"Can he be more specific?"

"Dark hair, dark skin, dark eyes, medium build."

"We need to find that car."

"I have my team searching, and I've contacted the police, so if they find it I'll know."

"Nico, get every man you have, and call in your backups. Spare no effort or expense. I want that car found. I want Ella found."

Distraught, Adam paced the floor. His wife was in the hands of enemies, and on the heels of the shock came panic. He had to stay calm, think clearly. Ella's safety could depend on it. No matter how he felt, Adam could not let emotion cloud his mind. Not now.

He dialed her cell number, knowing even as he did that it would be fruitless. Adam tried anyway but just got voicemail. The sound of her voice—*"This is Ella. Please leave a message"*—stabbed at his heart. *God. I'll find you, Ella. I'll do everything to find you. Hold on, amore mia. Please hold on.*

His phone vibrated again. This time it was a text message. The alarming words appeared on the screen: *We have her. Will call soon with demand.*

Merda, merda, merda! What he had feared was true. Ella had been abducted. Somehow, until he had evidence to confirm it, Adam had still held out hope that it wasn't the case. That it was just a misunderstanding, and his wife would return, explaining it all. Now he knew. There was no more messing around. This was serious business, and her life was at stake.

He checked for the source of the text but the information was blocked. They'd called his private cell, so the likely way they had gotten the number was out of Ella's phone. More confirmation they had her. As if he needed any. He should have never let her out of his sight.

Chapter 13

With Ella in grave danger, an effective strategy was required. Adam texted Quinn: *Urgent. I'll be right there.* And he had Miguel drive him back to the law office. He held his phone in his hand; it was vital that he not miss the ring when the crooks called back. The short ride downtown seemed to take forever.

The scenery of Rio sped by outside the windows. He'd seen it all his life, but now he barely saw it at all. Nothing seemed real. Disbelief that the woman he loved more than anything in this world had been taken from him wiped all, but that, from his mind. Adam could not even consider the possibility that he might lose her for good.

Quinn revealed no emotion, though Adam had no doubt the news had hit him hard.

"This is a kidnap situation. We will utilize experts, Adam. It's Ella's life at stake here."

Hearing Quinn say out loud what he could hardly face was like a punch to the gut. "Yes, the best. I figured you would know who to use."

"I'll coordinate with the insurance company."

"What does insurance have to do with it?"

"Most businesses that deal in international trade, such as you do, have coverage for bribery, ransom situations, all kinds of stuff. In many countries of the world, it has become more common to kidnap corporate employees and demand a ransom for their return. Precautions and procedures to avoid such are in place.

"But in your situation, it is different. This event may or may not be considered business related. It can be shown that Claudio pressured you before to turn over software you developed. And now this money demand comes in. I think a relationship could be demonstrated."

"Now that you mention it, I recall scanning that section of my policy. But how does that work?"

"Well, first of all, they don't cover any ransom demand. That will be up to you, to come up with the money."

"Money is not an issue. Whatever it takes to get Ella back. That's all I want."

"Yes, well, they do cover expenses—medical and so on. And before the marriage we added Ella to your policy, as you might remember. Since she travels everywhere with you. There will only be a claim if she is injured, or if you decide to file a claim for expenses you incur." Quinn paused before making his next point. "But here is the important thing."

Adam sat up straight, absorbing every detail. "What's that?"

"All big insurance companies have a team, trained and primed for conducting the negotiations. They also handle the logistics of the return of the victim in exchange for the funds. Whether this involves insurance or not, the team is for hire. I'll get a referral to make sure we have top-notch guys."

Adam knew for sure he wasn't trusting Ella's safe return to a bunch of men he didn't know. But their expertise in negotiating could be useful. "What do they do exactly?"

"They will be with us throughout the ordeal. I can get them here immediately. It's best if they are onsite when the demand comes in."

"Okay, check out that referral and get them over here. Tell them to hurry. I have no idea when these idiots are going to call."

Quinn made the call while Adam paced. He got a couple of referrals from another attorney he trusted, and called the most promising. The negotiators, used to short notice, arrived within the hour. Their responsiveness was impressive.

Adam looked them over as they sat around the table in the conference room. The three guys all looked like attorneys in their slacks and dress shirts. Nothing outstanding about any of them, but they were all business. Unemotional, detached, and dead calm, they took charge.

The tallest one, a lean guy with buzzed dark hair, spoke. "I know this is a bad situation for you, Mr. Bianci."

"Adam. If we are going to work together, there is no need for formality. This is about my wife."

"Yes...Adam. Let me tell you that things will progress rather rapidly."

"I want them to. I want this over as fast as possible. I want my wife back."

Another in the group, a brown-haired older man with a bit of weight on him, spoke up. "That is our job. To get your wife back, sir. And you have chosen well. We are good at our job. I hope you will trust us."

Adam was annoyed. "I trust nothing at the moment. The woman I love, my wife of less than a week, has been taken. I don't know where she is, or if she's all right. Or if I'll ever see her again. So, let's just get down to it, shall we?"

Quinn stood up. "Tell us what we can expect, Lawrence."

The tall one shifted from one foot to the other. "Okay, let me map this out for you. Normally, these situations are resolved...one way or the other...within seventy-two hours. Now, since you called us immediately, I have every reason to believe that we can be effective."

Adam cut him off. "What's the plan?"

"Do you have any idea what the demand will be?"

Adam shook his head. "No. But my father knows I'm

wealthy. That's no secret. And truthfully, if I could give him every dime to get Ella back, I would do so. But I still have no confidence Claudio would return her unharmed."

"I understand your concern. Let me say that whatever the demand, we will not agree to it."

Adam stood. "Yes, you will. I have no choice but to agree."

"No, and let me tell you why. If you want Ella back as soon as possible, it's imperative that we don't cave to their first demand."

Adam felt control slipping away, and he fought to stay calm. "How will you handle it, then?"

"We have to negotiate." Lawrence held his pen in one hand and glanced at his notebook on the table, as if reading a script.

Adam took a couple of steps toward the window and then returned. It was hard to keep still, hard to be pent up in the close quarters of the small room, with men he didn't know that well. But he had to trust Quinn's judgment. Clearly, the team had done this before, and their attitude inspired confidence.

Adam looked at Lawrence, unable to hide the challenge in his voice. "How do you propose to do that?"

"We always refuse the first demand."

"What if he threatens to kill her?"

"That's exactly what he *will* threaten. But he is bluffing. At least at first."

"How do you know he won't kill her if we piss him off?"

"There's very little chance. Ella is his leverage. If she is gone, the game is off. And the crooks have invested time and planning into this. They want the money."

"So why not just agree to the demand and get my wife back?"

"Big mistake. Fatal."

"Explain."

"If you agree to the ransom, no matter what the amount, Claudio will be angry with himself. Since you agreed so easily, he should have asked for more. And that is what he will do—call back with a higher demand. Which will only drag out the process. And the longer Ella is in their lair, the more danger she is in."

"It doesn't sound hopeful."

"If you let us handle it, the power will shift hands, and we will be in control. If your father decides to raise the demand, he will just keep doing so. He will bleed every cent out of you that he can. And whether you care about the money is not the point. The entire time we are bartering with him, Ella's chances of safe return are reduced."

"Fine. You convinced me. So when the phone rings, am I to understand you want to take the call?"

"Yes."

Adam placed his cell phone on the long table and glared at it. It was as if the device was the cause of his dilemma and shared responsibility for Ella's dire situation. "On one condition."

Lawrence raised his eyebrows, and his two associates looked over at Adam.

"I have top-of-the line software I developed to trace calls. It's faster and more effective than any on the market. Including what our law enforcement has access to. I've plugged it into my phone, and I intend to trace their location when they call. I want to be proactive, not just sit here and wait for them to return my wife."

Lawrence nodded, and the other two relaxed. "No problem."

While they all drank coffee, waiting for the call, Nico showed up. Adam went to the door and stood half in the hallway, but with the door open in case his phone rang.

"They found the car," Nico said. "It was abandoned less than a mile from the hotel. They were generally headed in the direction of the airport, but they could be anywhere. Since they switched vehicles, there's no way to tell. The police are dusting for prints, but I doubt it will do us any good. It's not like Claudio's accomplices have residential addresses. And by the time they are tracked down, if they can be, well…we don't have that kind of time."

Adam nodded. "We are waiting for the call to come in with the demand."

Nico said, "I'm going to work with the team, see what other leads we can come up with. I know Miguel drove you over, and there are two more guards in another vehicle out there with him. Will you be okay?"

"Yes, I'll let you know if I find out anything useful."

"I don't trust leaving anything to the local police. And it's not a big deal to them that a car was stolen and abandoned, especially now that the hotel has it back. Have you reported Ella missing?"

"Not yet. Right now I'm meeting with Quinn and the negotiations team we hired. If and when we report this to the authorities, I will let you know."

Nico started down the hall. "Then, based on the description we got, I'm going to ask around, see if anyone knows who he is. And I'll see if anyone else saw anything."

"Okay, call Quinn if you get a lead. My phone is kinda tied up at the moment."

The hours went by, and food was brought in. The others munched on their pizza and drank sodas. The aroma of baked crust filled the room, and the large pizzas were piled with ham, artichoke hearts, and mushrooms. Adam had no appetite; his stomach was in knots. He sipped coconut water to keep his strength up. The door to the conference room was propped open, and the men took excursions down the hall to stretch their legs.

The phone stayed with Adam wherever he went, and he was never far from the rest of the team. He looked out the windows at the darkness that had descended over the city and wondered where Ella was. And if she was okay. He figured that this early she would be all right—sort of. She had to be frightened out of her wits. And there was no guarantee how the creeps that had her would treat her.

He cursed his father over and over. It was just too much. Greed was one thing, and coming from Claudio, that did not surprise him. But kidnapping? The penalties for such an offense were severe. It was enough that his father had made enemies within his criminal circles and even had bad press, thanks to the exposure of his crimes in the papers.

But to incite the wrath of the government? Adam didn't think any bribery, especially from a small-time crook like his father, would assuage the heavy hand of the American government. Not once they learned one of their citizens, in Rio for her wedding, had been abducted. It was beyond comprehension. His father had lost his mind. There was no other explanation.

The time grew later, and the negotiations team brought in backups so they could go home to rest in rotation. It was vital that they stay sharp. Adam had no such luxury, and Quinn wouldn't hear of leaving. Cots were delivered so they could at least stretch out. But Adam and his attorney traded off on catnaps. They trusted no one more than they trusted each other and agreed that one of them would be awake at all times.

Rest didn't come easily for Adam. He drifted into a fitful sleep out of pure exhaustion, but had nightmares about what was going to happen to Ella. He woke no more refreshed than before he'd dozed off. The relationship with the negotiations team got cozy.

In close confines like they were, bored though concerned, there was little option but to chat to pass the time. Adam began to feel more comfortable with the group. Each man seemed competent in their own right, and the team appeared to truly care about the safe return of the hostage. But time would tell. The much-anticipated call had not yet come in.

Chapter 14

Ella woke into a nightmare. With her eyes still closed, unable to orient herself, she grasped for something familiar. A scratchy blanket prickled the backs of her legs and a cloying smell of dirty clothes and decay hit her nostrils. In a split second, it came back to her.

Her limbs felt weighted, her eyelids heavy. Nothing hurt, so that was good. But being thrown into an unfriendly environment, and cut off from those she was close to, was frightening. Determined not to give in to the terror, Ella slowly opened her eyes, and gazed up at a faded ceiling with peeling paint.

Testing her body, Ella moved her arms and legs. Everything seemed okay. She turned her head, spotted the closed door, and verified that she was alone. Easing into an upright position, she fought the lethargy that hung over her from the drug they'd injected. She needed to move around, get the feeling restored to her body.

Her muscles were like jelly, and her mind was dull. Walking the short distance from one wall to the other, she tried to assess her situation. The one window in the room was boarded over from the outside, so it was impossible to tell if it was day or night. The sedative had forced her into a deep unconsciousness, so she'd lost track of time.

How long had she been gone? Ella didn't know. By her level of hunger and thirst, she deduced it probably wasn't that long—not days, for sure. Maybe twenty-four hours. That was her best guess. The emptiness in her stomach confirmed she'd missed several meals, and since she hadn't taken the time for breakfast on the day of the abduction, hunger was pressing.

As if on cue, her stomach rumbled loudly, and Ella glanced at the door, anxious that any noise would bring her jailers to check on her. What she needed was a little time to think and plan. The situation wasn't good. Alone and unarmed, she was at their mercy, but she needed to do something to change the odds.

The small room was in an old building with walls that were sturdy enough to keep her in, but nailed together unevenly. The concrete floor was cracked and crumbling in places, with no carpet. The bed sagged badly and had no headboard or footboard. Light came from the one bulb hanging from the ceiling, probably controlled by the switch near the door. There was a tiny bathroom with no window and no door for privacy. It looked bare, other than a toilet and sink.

The atmosphere was depressing at best. Knowing South American ways, at least to some extent, Ella figured she was in a poor section of a city, maybe even a favela. There was no way to tell for sure. Noise rumbled outside at a distance—a variety of vehicle noises, shouting, and even a dog barking far off. But nothing close.

Oddly enough, she didn't hear any noise outside her door, so whoever was guarding her was awfully quiet. Possibly it was nighttime and they were sleeping, or there was one awake, quiet but alert. Not knowing how many were holding her hostage or what was going on outside the door to her small room was unnerving.

If she screamed, it was possible that no one would hear her—or, depending on the neighborhood, wouldn't care. The downside of calling for help was that she would immediately bring her guards into the room, and she was ill-prepared to deal with them. All she had was the shirt and shorts she'd worn, with her tennis shoes and socks still on.

Nico had kept her purse in the car; she'd only taken her cell and stuffed some cash in her pocket to go up and see Kaiyla. The thought of her friend sent a feeling of desperation pounding in her chest. What if she never saw her again? It was too sad to think about the possibility of never getting free, or that the last visit with her friend had been the final one.

The phone and cash were gone, obviously in the hands of the criminals. All her contacts were in that phone, making it easy enough to contact Adam on his private cell. That must be it: a ransom demand. There was no other reason they would have taken her. It was to put pressure on him for money.

It baffled her how they'd scooped her up so efficiently. Nico had not been far off, but he'd had no idea she'd taken a limo to coffee. But how had they? One way would have been to watch the hotel. After all, the wedding was no secret; it was even announced in the papers. And her family and friends had stayed at the Copacabana.

Patience paid off it seemed. All they needed to do was keep an eye on her family and friends, looking for the right opportunity. It had been safe when she was with Adam, so they had waited for a time when she was vulnerable. By her husband's side with bodyguards watching, had been no time to kidnap her.

The money was of primary importance, and Adam had access to it. So hurting him would be avoided. Better to get Ella when she was alone. Despite knowing about Claudio's demand, it had never seemed likely they would kidnap her. She'd met Adam's father under undesirable circumstances before, and he'd stated that he wouldn't do that.

Being a fugitive from a powerful government for abducting one of their citizens was something he would probably prefer to avoid. There had been no reason to do it at all. It would have made more sense to give Adam a chance to pay, but the amount of the demand or the details were never conveyed. Claudio's action seemed extreme.

Ella stretched then bent to touch her toes. It was important to stay flexible, as she might have to fight men that far outweighed her. Being light on her feet and making herself a more difficult target would be her strength. Whatever it took, she had to outsmart them and get free.

Adam must be worried sick. He would have no way of knowing where they'd taken her. In fact, she didn't even know if she was still in Rio. Since this was Claudio's plan, maybe he'd had his cohorts transport her to Paraguay, a safer turf for him. During the time she was out cold, they could have put her on a plane and she never would have known.

There was no other furniture in the room besides the bed and a dilapidated nightstand—no lamps, nothing. She searched for something to use as a weapon but came up dry. Discouraged, Ella dropped onto the bed, unable to push away her longing to be with Adam.

She'd screwed up. Day after day, an army of security hovered close to protect them. Though she didn't foresee any physical threat, it was smart not to allow the bad guys access. Then, off guard briefly, excited to see Kaiyla and tell her about Santa Teresa, she'd failed to ensure Nico was with her.

It hadn't seemed important at the time. Just back from a three-day trip with her husband and still emotionally high from the wedding, Ella had felt untouchable. Life was too good to conceive of bad. And that had been her weakness. Irresponsibly, frivolously, she'd gone down the street for coffee, never dreaming she was walking right into their hands.

The driver had waited for them. A thought slapped her into awareness. When they got back to the hotel limo, it hadn't been the same driver. He'd removed his hat, but that wasn't all. At the time she'd brushed it aside, but the man had had different mannerisms. Somehow he'd commandeered the vehicle and gotten rid of the hotel employee.

If she'd been sharper, more aware of what was happening, Ella would have known that and never gotten in the limo. *Stupid, stupid. I was just so stupid.* And now it was too late. She was putting Adam through hell. And worse than that, if things didn't turn out well, she might never see him again. The burden of her error was heavy on her shoulders. Ella slumped, placing her head in her hands.

The tiny room was claustrophobic, and the degraded environment with the rancid smell overwhelmed her. There was no doubt in her mind that Adam would do everything he could to get her back. But what if he couldn't? Paying the money wouldn't be an issue. She knew her husband well enough to know the money meant nothing to him without her.

Even so, there was no guarantee they would return her to him. Claudio was a druggie, erratic in his behavior, and less than rational in his thoughts. Possibly, it wasn't solely about the money. Revenge might be part of the picture. If he was resentful over Adam's prior attack and having to flee to Paraguay, Claudio might retaliate. And what better way to get back at his son than take away what he loved most?

The more she thought, the more desperate Ella felt. This wasn't going to be easy. She would need to push aside her regrets and her fears. Until she was free, what mattered was staying sharp and being strong. There might be only one opportunity to escape, and she was determined not to miss it.

Footsteps creaked on sagging wood like someone walking upstairs. That was a clue. Maybe they were downstairs, which was why she was unable to hear them. The doorknob jiggled, as if a key had been inserted, then turned. Ella held her breath, clutching at the blanket for defense, having no other. A tall, thin man stepped inside. By his skin tone, Ella guessed he was Hispanic, but it was difficult to tell. He wore a ski mask, which gave him a terrifying appearance.

Due to the disguise, she didn't know his hair color, but she could see his dark eyes. Dressed in tattered jeans and an old shirt, he strode over to her in a commanding fashion. He held a tray of food. "Jantar," he said, and placed the tray on the bed next to her. He smelled as if he hadn't bathed recently and his clothes needed washing.

Ella recognized the Portuguese word for *dinner*, and nodded. "Obrigada." It couldn't hurt to be friendly, and maybe she could gain support from one or more of the crooks. They were people, after all, and if they felt kindly towards her they'd be less inclined to see harm come to her.

"Que horas são?" Clearly this one wasn't easily softened up. Her question about the time was met with no response.

The man turned and started for the door.

"What are you going to do with me?"

He showed no sign if he understood English, and Ella's knowledge of Portuguese was limited. With a nod toward her tray, indicating she should eat, he opened the door and left. The food didn't smell bad, but it didn't smell good either. It wasn't a dish she recognized, and she guessed it was just whatever they had, mixed together.

Ella balked at eating, uncertain if they would try to poison her. But then it was too early for such rash action. Their first step would be to use her for bait to get the money. Until that happened, they'd need her in good shape. After that, well, it was hard to say. It was important not to allow herself to weaken, either mentally or physically.

Lifting the warm plate onto her lap, Ella looked at it closer. The meat was probably beef, since there wasn't much likelihood of them affording the rarer types. There were some big chunks of potato stirred in a sauce with kale. It could be worse. One bite at a time, she choked it down. There was no way she'd take a chance of failing to escape due to a weakened state from malnutrition.

As it was, Ella had no idea how long they planned to keep her. Or how long it would take Adam to find her, if he did at all. Stopping halfway through the suspect meal, Ella reached for the water to wash it down. There was no way she could eat another bite. Her stomach was objecting as it was. Nibbling at the dry bread that accompanied her meal, she tried to think.

The man had said *dinner*, confirming that it was evening. Or might be, anyway. His nationality suggested they were still in Brazil. In Paraguay, the common language was Spanish, a language that Ella didn't speak at all. Fortunately, she'd learned some conversational Portuguese, and now hoped it would be an advantage.

She wondered if Claudio would show up or stay safe in Paraguay. It puzzled her that he'd garnered enough help to pull off a kidnapping. But then, if he had revealed how wealthy his son was and had offered them a cut, it would be more than enough incentive. The picture looked bleak. If Ella knew one thing, she knew that it was easy to get lost in the bowels of Rio.

The favelas, or poor areas of the city, were mazes controlled by gangs. In that environment, nobody would pay much attention to a band of crooks out for ransom. Much worse had been done in the favelas, and the crime rate was high. Somehow, she'd have to fend for herself. But *how* was the question.

Chapter 15

It had been less than twenty-four hours since Ella's abduction, and already the stuffy conference room felt like a jail cell. If Adam didn't get some fresh air soon, he was going to lose what sanity he had left. Spending the night wondering if his wife was okay, and whether they'd harmed her, was agonizing.

When he'd been awake, Adam had talked to the negotiators. Their questions had been answered without hesitation, as he was willing to do anything that might help. Lawrence had more questions than the others, and covered things about Ella. Knowing her personality, strengths, and weaknesses could be of use when it came time for the exchange. Even beforehand, in haggling over the ransom.

Everything about Claudio was relevant—his vices, his enemies, even his friends, though Adam doubted he had any. One never knew which bit of information could be vital. Nothing was too trivial. Some of it was assumption on Adam's part. He hadn't seen his father in years.

But some things don't change, and he was certain his father's addiction to heavy drugs motivated much of his action. It piqued Lawrence's interest when Adam discussed his father's inclination for revenge and detailed what had gone on before. Money was primary, but there was probably a secondary intent to get back at his son for the way he'd been brushed aside before.

In private, Adam had talked with Quinn and decided not to go to the authorities just yet. Both knew any governmental body was slow to act, and there was a possibility their involvement might make things worse. They could still report the kidnapping later, if it came to that. But Adam knew that the first forty-eight hours would be crucial, and he didn't want to deal with the police.

He had all he could do to focus on the matter at hand. He figured if he and Quinn couldn't succeed in the exchange of money for his wife, especially with the best negotiators in the trade, then neither could the police. Plus, it wasn't a priority for them like it was for Adam. This wasn't just one more crime buried in a pile of cases; it was the only thing that mattered, his sole focus.

Lawrence, to his credit, had stayed the night and was still with them, though Adam suspected he would soon accept a replacement so he could go home and get some rest. The other two men left before morning, and two new ones replaced them. All notes taken in interviewing Adam were secured in a laptop, and the new staff reviewed them in preparation.

At dawn, fresh coffee was brought in, along with crusty bread, ham, cheese, and fresh fruit. This time, Adam ate some of the bread and ham with his coffee. He needed to stay sharp, so appetite or not, food was essential. Whatever it took to keep a clear head, he would do. This was no time to fall apart.

Before the food was cleared, Adam's cell phone rang. They'd stared at it for so many hours that when the shrill sound reverberated against the conference table, everyone froze. Except for Lawrence. He remained cool, and if Adam hadn't known he was about to take a ransom call, he would have thought his wife was calling about their dinner plans.

Seated in one of the padded office chairs, Lawrence leaned back, his wrinkled shirt the only sign that he'd had little sleep. Adam wished he could hear the conversation on speaker phone, but he knew if the crooks were aware there were so many listening, so many men present, they might react badly.

"Hello," Lawrence said, trying English first. The text the day before had been in English, even though Claudio knew his son grew up speaking both Italian and Portuguese. Another mystery. Possibly he thought English would have more impact, knowing Adam spoke English in most situations.

Without revealing anything in his expression, Lawrence shifted into Portuguese. Every man on the team was multilingual, as being able to speak to criminals in their language was a necessity. There was no other sound in the room besides the senior negotiator's voice bantering with whoever was on the other end of the line.

The conversation seemed long, though it concluded promptly. When Lawrence put the phone down, he looked up confidently. "It went as expected."

"Who was it? What did he say?" Adam was impatient. He'd heard only one side of the conversation. Taking control, Lawrence had explained who he was, and had in no uncertain terms declined the demand. He'd made an offer of his own—take it or leave it—and disconnected the call.

"Portuguese, though I doubt it was your father. It would make more sense for him to have one of his accomplices make the demand. But I wouldn't have been able to tell anyway, even if I did know your father's voice. They used a voice disguiser, which is a common practice."

Quinn leaned on the table. "A computer-generated voice?"

"Yes, and the number he was calling from was blocked. It's likely a disposable phone. I informed him that I was the negotiator. I doubt that surprised him too much. In the practice of kidnapping for ransom, negotiators are a popular occurrence. I don't know whether Claudio has done this before, but whoever handled that call seemed well versed."

Adam spoke directly to Lawrence. "What was the amount of the demand?"

"The amount was conveyed in Brazilian currency: one hundred million reas."

Adam did a quick calculation in his head. "That's over forty-one million dollars."

"And a ridiculous demand. Which I told him. My reply was ten million reas, take it or leave it. And I hung up."

Although Adam was not concerned with the amount of ransom—as long as it meant the safe return of his wife—he was nervous about pushing the kidnappers, knowing that with enough provocation they would harm her. "So you think they will accept a figure just over four million dollars?"

"I know it. We just have to let them know we are in control here, and need to treat this like any other business transaction. They will stall to make us worry. But they will call back."

Adam pulled his laptop closer and clicked away on the keys. "Let's see what we have here, on their location." His software had worked as predicted, and a map was displayed with a red mark to indicate where the call came from. "The airport."

Quinn slid closer to take a look.

Adam was already using Quinn's cell to contact Nico. He relayed what he'd learned and said, "Check it out."

Lawrence shrugged. "I doubt that is where they have Ella. They have to be keeping her somewhere private, not parading her around in public."

"I agree," Adam said. "But maybe we can get a lead, or pick up one of them. We have to try." He spoke boldly, though he was disappointed that his trace hadn't led to their hideaway. It was too much to hope for.

Adam went to the window and looked out on the thriving city of Rio. Everyone was going about their daily routine, unaware that Adam was having the worst day of his life, and that his wife may be suffering untold indecencies. It was as if he lived in a world adjacent to theirs, one they had no awareness of.

He raked his hand through his hair, bereft without Ella. It felt as though his heart had been ripped out and stomped on. If possible, he would trade places with her, let Claudio do his worst to his own son but leave his wife out of it. But that wasn't the reality.

Ella was alone, scared, and uncertain whether a successful rescue would be achieved. Adam knew she trusted him and would count on him. He couldn't fail her. He couldn't face the future without her. Praying they were treating her reasonably, and hadn't harmed her, Adam turned to face the room.

Adam studied Lawrence, who sat relaxed in his chair as if he handled ransom calls as a steady diet and could not be flustered. "What next?"

"We wait," Lawrence responded with no hesitation. "My guess is we won't have to wait long. I've been doing this job for a while, and the guy struck me as amateur. He won't have the patience."

"And when he calls back?"

"We wrap it up; seal the agreement of the funds in exchange for the victim." The instant he said it, Lawrence flinched. It was the first time Adam had seen him do so. Calling Ella a victim was a slip, and not the verbiage to use to keep your client calm.

Adam paid little attention to the other two negotiators. One, in a beige polo shirt, was clearly an assistant. He typed away on the laptop, recording everything as it transpired. The other one had been introduced as the insurance company representative. The well-dressed man, groomed and professional, was there to observe, and could also make decisions on behalf of the company.

Right then, both Quinn and Adam couldn't have cared less about insurance. The company couldn't do anything to bring Ella back, nor prevent harm from coming to her. But as long as they were unobtrusive, Adam allowed their representative to stay put. He had access to the team of negotiators, which was what counted.

Minutes ticked by slowly, and everyone tried to divert their attention away from the phone but couldn't help glancing at it expectantly. Thankfully, the waiting didn't extend into another night, which would have been intolerable considering it was only mid-morning. As Lawrence predicted, the crooks were low on patience and called back within the hour.

Adam listened intently while Lawrence went over the ransom details as if speaking to a child. He explained in a calm tone that funds were not liquid, that AB Software had debts, that the economy had been tight. As the expert negotiator impressed upon the criminal the difficulty of accessing such a large sum of money, Adam found *himself* believing that he was close to broke and could not get cash quickly even though Ella's life depended on it.

All night, Adam had been racking his brain to come up with a way to outwit the crooks. They had brawn and violence on their side. But the one thing Adam had—the thing that had always been his salvation—was his intelligence. More specifically, his adeptness with software and talent with computers.

Quickly he scribbled on a piece of paper, one word in large letters: *WIRE*

He shoved it over to Lawrence, who nodded. From the course of the conversation, it appeared the negotiator had convinced the evildoer on the other end of the line that the ransom offer was firm, and he should jump at the chance to get it. In fluent Portuguese, he advised him, like a father sharing wisdom with a son, that it was smart to take money he could get quickly over a larger sum he would never see.

Details were ironed out without hesitation, and Lawrence informed him that the funds would be wired. An account number would need to be provided; they could text it as soon as secured. But the absolute soonest the funds could be transferred was forty-eight hours. Beaten down by Lawrence's lecture on the hardship of getting a large sum of money on short notice, the crook did not argue.

The call was over. Everyone in the room looked up, anxious for closure.

Lawrence stood, stretching as if sitting and lecturing so long had made his muscles stiff. "It's agreed. He conceded to our amount. And will provide the account number where we are to wire the funds."

Adam interrupted. "Why forty-eight hours?"

"Same reasoning as before. If it's too easy to get, he will be inclined to ask for more. But to pick too long a deadline would discourage him, and might prompt an adverse reaction. Forty-eight hours is ideal."

Quinn spoke as if reading Adam's mind. "And what's the procedure to get Ella back?"

Lawrence stood facing them with his hands clasped together. "They will let us know where and when to pick her up—once they see the funds. And, as a guarantee that she will be unharmed until then, I told him it was mandatory for her husband to speak with her before we press the button for the funds transfer."

Adam had never trusted his father, and this occasion was no exception. "How do I know they won't just record her voice to deceive me?"

"Because you will ask her something that only she knows. Only Ella will be able to give you the answer; it's nothing they could pre-record. That will be your verification she is unharmed."

Satisfied with that, Adam leaned back in his chair and took a deep breath. So far, so good, but there was still a long way to go. Hashing out an agreement about the ransom total was the easy part; getting Ella back would prove more formidable. The negotiators may have experience in doing clean deals with kidnappers, but they hadn't dealt with Claudio.

For his father, this wasn't business, it was personal. Adam had witnessed the cruelty with which Claudio could treat others, even assaulting Serena, his own wife.

Nothing was beyond his ability when it came to destruction, especially if he saw an advantage. And getting back at Adam for prior mistreatment, and for being thwarted in his evil schemes, would be reason enough.

Chapter 16

Quinn pushed back his chair and stood. His brown eyes revealed exhaustion he must have felt, but his tone of voice conveyed determination. "That's it for now. We have forty-eight hours, so it's advisable to break up and reconvene very early the day after tomorrow."

Picking up his notebook and pushing back from the conference table, Lawrence said, "Agreed. We will have a team here around the clock. Our replacements are on the way. If the phone rings, the call will be handled as you would expect. And the caller did stress no police. Where do we stand on that?"

Quinn looked at Adam, deferring the decision to him.

Standing, anxious to get out of the confines of the enclosed room, Adam replied without hesitation. "No police. I don't think they would be of use at this point. Things are moving rapidly. If we have to call them in later, so be it. But not now."

Lawrence nodded, showing no surprise over the decision not to involve the authorities.

Adam had more to say, though. "What are the chances they will call early? Try to speed the process?"

Shaking his head, Lawrence said, "Almost zero. I've never had it happen. They want you working on getting that money. And they want you worried about Ella. It's better for them to stall. It's more advantageous to delay your verification that your wife is okay, kind of their ace in the hole. They know you will be doing everything you can to get the funds on time. We can assume there will not be any call tonight or tomorrow. However, they may call earlier on the morning of the deadline. I expect their patience will be worn thin by then."

Everyone nodded, agreeing with that assessment, and the group dispersed, moving slowly from prolonged hours of sitting. Except for Adam. Speed was of the essence, and every second counted. He followed his attorney into his office. "I don't trust that Ella will be returned safely."

Quinn nodded. "We know your father; they don't. He doesn't play fair, never has."

"True. I want you to keep an eye on things here. Go home and get some rest, but check in with them. Let me know if there's anything new. You can contact Nico; that would probably be best since it's unlikely I'll see any email. And my phone isn't leaving that conference room."

"Yes, don't concern yourself about the negotiating team. I'll handle that. Keep me advised of any strategy you are going to employ."

"Definitely. And if you think of an angle, let me know. We need to take charge of ensuring Ella's safety."

After exiting the building, Adam breathed in the fresh morning air. It was a relief not to be cooped up with a bunch of men under stressful circumstances. He thought of Ella, knowing it was unlikely she breathed outside air along with him. Adam's heart ached, and the empty pit in his chest made him want to curl up in agony.

That wasn't an option. The woman he loved, more than anything, needed him. Pushing aside his heavy emotion, he strode to the car where Miguel waited to take him home. Likely his loyal driver had slept in the car. As they pulled out to the street, Adam noticed the vehicle with his other two guards followed.

He was safe enough at the moment. Harming him would only defeat the purpose of the kidnapping, and lose the ransom for the crooks. Until the money was in their hands, Adam could move unrestricted, as long as he didn't go to the authorities. There was some comfort knowing they would keep Ella unharmed until he spoke to her just prior to the funds transfer.

But he trusted nothing. Not when it came to Claudio. On the way, Adam tried to clear his head and come up with a way to find Ella. It wasn't something he could do alone; he would need to call upon his allies. Once he was home, Miguel left for a welcome break, but fresh bodyguards arrived. Yet Adam paid little attention; his mind was on one thing only.

He had an idea and needed to think it through. After stripping off his clothes, Adam headed for the shower. Despite the air conditioning in the office building, it had been a sweaty night. He needed to freshen up. Calling on a friend was best done from a position of strength, though the subject concerned his vulnerability.

Anyone that knew him well had no doubt Ella was his soft spot. And now that was being used against him. Whatever it took, Adam was going to turn the tables, and he would get his wife back. One thing the bad guys didn't have on their side was the power of love. They had only hate. But Adam knew they had made a serious error when coming between him and the woman he loved. They'd turned him into a ruthless enemy, more motivated than a band of criminals out for stolen wealth.

The hot water felt good, and Adam let it pour over him while he mulled his idea over. It was only part of the solution, but it was a start. Clean and revitalized from the shower, he put on some khakis and a linen shirt. The usual shorts and T-shirt wouldn't do, as he needed to be prepared to go anywhere at a moment's notice.

What the next few hours held, Adam wasn't sure. But it would be a volatile couple of days. Dressed and groomed, he went to the kitchen to look for something to satisfy his grumbling stomach. In the refrigerator, he found some fish and vegetables Ella had made the first night home from Santa Teresa.

She liked to cook, especially for him. Looking at the leftovers of the meal prepared with care, Adam got choked up. *Amore mia. I will see you again. No one can take you from me.*

He heated the dish and ate while he thought. Things were coming together in his mind. Finally, with space to think, Adam began to feel more positive about the dire circumstances. Taking a swig of beer, he washed down the delicious morsels, feeling better.

Stronger, he went out to the pool and looked out at the bay. It was a beautiful, pleasant day with a light breeze. A day for soaking up the sun at the beach with his wife. He longed to hold her and tell her how much he loved her. Memories of her laughter, her womanly scent, and her intimate touch flooded back. Everything he saw, everywhere he looked reminded him of Ella.

He gazed across the water toward the sprawling city in the distance. Ella was out there, somewhere. And he was going to find out where. His despicable father would not get away with this crime. The key was finding his wife before it was too late. And the minutes ticked by, time quickly running out.

Nico arrived with an update. "I have a team at the airport, but so far, nothing. Galeão is like a small city. At an airport that large, it's easy to get lost. I doubt we will find the man that called from there."

"I'm sure he's left, and probably looks like hundreds of others in the throngs of travelers. Most likely the next call will be placed from a different location. These guys are idiots, but I think even they would know better than to frequent the same places."

Holding up a phone, Nico nodded.

"Ah, great. I need a phone."

"This is disposable, for temporary use. It will be good enough for the next couple of days."

Adam held the phone like it was a lifeline. "Anything from the hotel?"

"Nothing. No one saw the crook that stole the limo. We are still interviewing staff, but I'm not hopeful. My guess is that he never went to the hotel, just scooped the limo right off the street. The new driver believed he was his replacement."

"Yes, I'm sure that's how it went down."

"And trying to find witnesses in the shops along the street near the coffee shop is an exercise in futility."

"I'm not surprised. This is Rio. Anyone who did see the vehicle might not even be here anymore, considering how many tourists fill the streets near Copacabana. Besides, it was just one more limo among many others."

Nico nodded. "We did find the counter clerk at the coffee shop who remembers your wife and her friend. He was a young man and he says he noticed two beautiful women chatting away with each other, even describing Ella's big brown eyes and Kaiyla's striking blond hair."

Adam's heart fell. Just hearing mention of Ella before the disastrous incident racked him with emotional pain. "And did he see them leave?"

"As you might imagine, he did watch them walk out—enjoying the view, you might say. But it was a busy morning and he didn't see anything after they left the shop."

"Disappointing. We need something solid, something we can use."

"We will get it. We won't give up." Nico stood at attention, ever the professional. "What next?"

"I want you to drive me to see Gustavo. It's time to lean on our allies. Let's start with him."

The office building where Vinicius Gustavo Cardoso ran the operations for his foundation was not far from the law office where Adam had spent the night. The former drug lord was now respectable, and his reputation for assisting drug-addicted criminals to find a more legitimate lifestyle had earned him much respect.

Inside, the building was like any other, if more sparsely furnished. It made a statement that every dime went to help those in need, and not for any luxury of accommodations. Adam had no question that Gustavo would see him. Over the months, both Adam and his wife had supported his goodwill projects, and they'd become friends.

The receptionist buzzed them in through a bullet-proof glass barrier. Not everyone supported Gustavo in his desire to leave a life of crime. And some enemies would relish the chance to thwart him in his goal. He fearlessly continued in his mission, but took precautions against those that would stop him.

Nico walked down the hall, just behind Adam, and they entered the modest office. Sitting behind a narrow wooden desk, Gustavo still fit the image of an underworld drug baron. The dark skin of his forearms was covered with elaborate tattoos. His chest and shoulders were thickly muscled, and his dark hair was shaved close to the head.

"Alô," Adam said.

Gustavo motioned for them to sit. "Nico. Adamo. Como posso ajudá-lo?" he asked, getting down to business.

While Nico sat quietly observing, Adam launched into the story of Ella's abduction, speaking Portuguese to his friend. He overlooked no detail, wanting Gustavo to have the full picture. It was possible he would think of something Adam had not, and there was no doubt he would be willing to help if he could.

When Adam was done, Gustavo sat thoughtfully, his fingers together like a steeple under his chin. His dark eyes gave nothing away.

Adam waited. Nico said nothing.

Then Gustavo asked directly, "O que posso fazer?"

Though he asked *What can I do?* Adam suspected he had some ideas. But this was Ella they were talking about, and he would follow Adam's guidance on how to proceed.

The importance of the situation demanded a forthright approach. It was no time for polite discourse. Adam told Gustavo that he wanted him to find out about Claudio.

Though he'd fled to Paraguay the last time they'd had him on the run, now he was conducting his sordid affairs within the boundaries of Brazil. It seemed unusually bold, and there was little time to unravel the mystery.

Ella's life depended on gaining more information about Claudio's activities, and who his accomplices were. No detail was insignificant; anything might prove to be vital. Adam did not personally have connections to the underworld where his father found support. For that, he needed to count on Gustavo.

At first, Adam's friend claimed he had given up that life, turned away from crime. But he didn't refuse to help, giving the opening Adam needed. He told Gustavo that he understood how he felt about drug gangs and the criminals that profited within them. But he also knew that Gustavo was a man that always kept his finger on the pulse of that world.

It made sense to keep your eye on the enemy and avoid being caught unsuspecting. Adam was sure Gustavo had maintained connections and had friends that he could count on to keep him enlightened on anything vital. He told him that he knew his information channels had not dried up. And for Ella's sake, it was vital that Gustavo glean any information he could. It might make the difference.

Adam knew how Gustavo felt about Ella. Ever since the day she'd joined the tour to the favelas for the sole purpose of meeting him, he'd admired her courage. On the one hand, he cut an imposing figure, one that others feared, and it worked to his advantage. But it also severed his closeness with others. Too often they trembled in his presence and were too timid to speak their mind.

Not so for Ella, who had boldly asked for his help, and even contributed the last of her savings to his worthy reform cause. He never forgot that, and thought very highly of Adam's courageous wife. There was no question he would do what he could to ensure her safe return. As Adam expected, he pledged to do as asked. But he couldn't guarantee that he would uncover anything useful.

"Eu farei o meu melhor," he said, letting Adam know he would do his best.

Gustavo was not a man to be hugged, or kissed on the cheek, in the common Brazilian show of affection. Too much rough living had hardened his edges. But the warmth he felt for Adam and his concern for Ella came through in his firm handshake. Before leaving, Adam wrote down the number to his new cell phone and asked his friend to call with any news.

Back in the car, Nico asked, "What do you think?"

"The man is a legend the way he rose to the top of the criminal world and took charge of a prominent group. There's no one in the underworld of Rio, and maybe beyond, that hasn't heard of Gustavo Cardoso. His network is like a web, winding through the favelas, areas where you or I would fear to tread. If anyone can find something out, it's him."

"I hope it's in time."

"Yes, I pray that it will be."

Chapter 17

Despite thinking for hours, which was all she had to do, Ella couldn't see a way out. It was difficult to imagine a way for Adam to rescue her, and she had no confidence they would release her once the money was paid. They wore masks to disguise their faces so she would not be able to identify them, and they were cold toward her.

There was no reason for them to let her go. Fairness was unlikely a part of their moral code, and what motivation would they have once they had the ransom? In some areas of the city, Ella could disappear without a trace. Maybe she'd never be found. The thought made her shudder.

On the plus side, they did feed her regularly, but she suspected they did that so she would give a good report to Adam. The criminal mind was beyond her full understanding, but she knew Adam. And she was certain he would demand to speak to her before releasing the funds.

With a guarantee that she was unharmed, he'd have no further reason to delay payment. It would be a few days at best, but Ella had lost track of time. With no visible sunrise or sunset, she could only measure her days by the meals they served. But since they were usually the same thing, it was hard to differentiate breakfast from dinner. Except they served hot coffee once a day and it made sense to do that at the first meal.

So Ella decided to tell time based on the arrival of her daily coffee. And it had been served once, so she guessed she had been in confinement for one day. It seemed so much longer, especially with nothing to do and endless time to worry. To occupy her mind, she began doing exercises. It would keep her body strong.

When she tired of that, Ella would sit on her forlorn bed and work on a fictional story in her head. Fretting incessantly about the kidnapping was unhealthy; it made her dull and burdened with concern. But when she got home, Ella planned to start on her next romance novel. Going over the plot in her head put her thoughts on a more positive course and kept her sharp. The distraction was welcome.

The only trouble with that was whenever she thought about the characters in her love story, she thought of Adam. And she missed him so desperately. It would have been bad enough being away from him for days, but what made it worse was not being sure she'd ever see him again. Still, she persevered, determined to seize the opportunity to escape should one become available.

It was a different man who had served breakfast, and a third, that had served lunch. That meant a minimum of three in the gang that held her. She wondered if Claudio were there, downstairs, too cowardly to face her. However, she thought it more likely he'd stayed in Paraguay and let his accomplices do his dirty work.

If he did show up, she would know it. The one time she'd met him had been under bad circumstances. As was his habit, he had threatened her, and his son, as well. Ella would never forget his voice. It was distinctive, raspy and sort of gravelly. The sound was forever in her memory. Adam's father could wear a mask, but if he spoke she'd know it was him.

So far, she had not heard any talking. However many

there were on site, they stayed downstairs. Only when mealtime arrived did one of them clomp up the noisy stairs to serve her. With the language barrier, she'd been unable to get them talking, and her efforts to soften their feelings toward her had failed.

Ella considered making a break for it when the door to her room opened, but decided against it. She saw no way to get free from so many men, and they might injure her during any escape attempt, putting her in a worse condition for any future rescue. No, she wouldn't risk it. It was better to play it smart.

Convinced they'd make a mistake, she observed everything. They were only an amateur bunch of criminals; they'd mess up sooner or later. And when they did, Ella would exploit their weakness. For now, she memorized the clothes they wore, how they walked, their mannerisms. And she looked for clues in her room as to where they might be.

It wasn't looking good, though. Locked in a small room with no windows, Ella's resources were limited. When desperation threatened to overcome her, she fell onto the creaky bed and closed her eyes. In her mind, she could feel the sun and hear the ocean. Remembering the swells at the beach near their home, she felt the sensation of being thrown to the crest of a wave and riding under the curl. Surfing had always been her escape, and it was again.

*****

Nico drove back to the beach house with Adam lost in thought. "Do you think she is still in Rio?"

Adam considered the question. "I've been thinking about that. If they want to do a trade, it would be more convenient to keep her close. That would make sense. But if they don't plan on releasing her, it wouldn't matter."

Nico glanced at him. "There's another reason."

Adam shifted in his seat. "What's that?"

"It's not easy to transport a woman across the border to Paraguay. You can hide stolen goods, drugs, and other things in clever ways. But a person is different. Especially an American. She would stand out."

Seeing the certainty in Nico's expression, Adam relaxed just a little. "Yes, you have a good point."

Nico continued, further supporting his argument. "I don't think they'd risk it. Their primary aim is to get the ransom money. And your father has no purpose in having Ella near him. I see no reason for Claudio to personally come to Rio. Everything points against it. But I don't think they've taken her far."

Adam rubbed his temples, frustrated with his inability to glean substantial clues about where his wife was being held. "That's the thing. We could be within a couple of miles of where they have her hidden and not know it. This city is like a maze, particularly when you get into the poorer areas."

"Unfortunately, that's true. There are too many options. We need a way to narrow it down." Nico signaled and changed lanes, then glanced back at Adam.

Looking straight ahead, out at the crowded streets of Rio, Adam spoke. "There is another thing we need."

Nico raised his eyebrows. "Which is?"

"Reinforcements. Once we find out where she is, we will need to get her free. I will feel better having some ruthless soldiers on our side." He looked over at Nico.

"Who do you suggest?"

Adam began dialing his phone. "I haven't needed an army before, but now that I do, I think Taiz is the man to call."

Since Claudio had betrayed Taiz Mezzanetti and incurred his wrath, he'd made a formidable enemy. The sentiment in Rio for some criminals was that going legit was an advantage. That was true for Taiz. He had modified his gambling operations to run them within the confines of local laws, and had found new ways to make them lucrative.

One of the ways had been to purchase gambling software Adam had designed. It made online gambling a reality, and Taiz had instantly become a business partner. Since then, he'd been friendlier, though he would still be a fierce enemy if crossed. Adam knew better than to go against him, and never had any desire to do so.

Quite the opposite—he was content to maintain the relationship, and valued the friendship. Chasing after Claudio when he'd fled to Paraguay hadn't held much interest for Taiz. Though Adam's father owed him quite a bit of money from gambling debts, Taiz had little reason to hope it would ever be paid.

Claudio just wasn't worth the trouble, and if he stayed out of the way, Taiz would have written him off. But he hadn't. Adam's father was looking for a big payday from his son, and the outstanding gambling debts would be of interest once again. Though Taiz had endorsed a life of crime earlier in his history, he hated cowards. And he thought of Claudio as nothing more than a cheap crook, and a dishonest one at that.

Often Adam spoke to Taiz, mostly about business matters, sometimes to share a few personal tidbits—though the former criminal kept most things private out of habit. After a couple of rings, Taiz picked up. Adam was one of the few men who had his private number.

"Olá."

"Taiz, it's Adam. I'm on a different phone; I'll be using this number for the next couple of days. There's an urgent situation I need to speak to you about."

"What's happened?"

Once again, Adam relayed the details of the abduction. This time it wasn't so much information he sought, as support.

Taiz responded as soon as Adam finished the story. "Your father doesn't learn, does he?"

"No, he refuses to change his ways."

After a deep sigh, his friend continued. "Well, he was lucky I let him go the first time. Now I see it was an error. I should have had my men take care of him for good. Now he's back, thinking he can win this game. No doubt he plans to take the ransom and disappear. He still owes me a sizeable sum. Plus, it aggravates me that he had the gall to detain Ella."

Adam glanced at Nico, who was listening to every word. "I'm sure he didn't plan on splitting the money with you."

After a short, derisive laugh, Taiz said, "No, I'm sure he hired crooks to handle the kidnapping. I wonder if he's even told them how much money is involved."

"Well, at least one knows—the one making the demand," Adam said.

"Over a voice distorter. What makes you think that's not Claudio?"

It was a legitimate question but Adam was pretty certain of what he'd observed. "Just the way he's approaching it, what he's saying. I know him too well. There's nothing of my father in that man's demeanor."

"You would know. So, what's the plan?"

Adam ran his fingers through his hair, wishing he had more to offer. "I'm working on that, trying to get information. I need to find out where they are holding her."

"I'll check around, but I'll have to keep it quite. We don't want to alarm them."

"No we don't, which is why I'm not bringing the authorities into it," Adam said.

"You're smart not to."

"But I need your help, Taiz."

"Ask."

Taking a deep breath, Adam plunged ahead. "Well, when we do find her—and we will—I need to free her. I will need a team of tough, savvy men. I have my own bodyguards, but as you and I know, criminals have different ways of fighting. I need men who know the ropes and will come through for me. Things might get violent."

Taiz didn't hesitate. "I have the men you need. Just give me the word when you are ready. But I have one question. Suppose Claudio is among them. He is your father, and I cannot guarantee he won't get hurt. Or even that he would survive the skirmish. Can you deal with that?"

Adam was caught off guard. It was his father. Could he launch an attack that might hurt him? Could Adam witness his death, or could he do it himself if it came to that? Oddly enough, he felt no sympathy, as a son should. He felt nothing in his heart for the man. Even worse than all the oppression Adam had suffered by his hand, or that his mother had endured, now the soulless shell of a man had taken Ella. And the possibility existed that he would do away with her.

Adam spoke with confidence. "My father is of no concern to me. I want Ella back. If Claudio is a casualty of this battle, it is his own doing. It's as much as he deserves." Then he had another thought. "I think you are developing a conscience, Taiz."

The sound of his deep belly laugh boomed through the phone. "You flatter me. However, I take friendship seriously. You can count on having the men you need. You have my word."

The phone went dead, and Adam gazed out the window at the steep hillsides covered with makeshift buildings, the favelas. Ella was in there somewhere, he was sure of it. If only he could get to her faster. The hard part was waiting.

Part of his plan was getting back at the criminals. They couldn't just show up, threatening and bullying, kidnap his wife, and walk away with millions. It wasn't right. But a lot depended on what Gustavo could find out, and on Taiz coming through with the muscle they needed. One more day, but it seemed like an eternity.

Chapter 18

The room was dark, with no outside illumination available. Ella was forced to keep the one tiny overhead bulb lit all through the night, as the pitch black was terrifying. Dread of how long she might be kept in captivity unsettled her. Tossing and turning on the narrow bed, she tried to keep her nightmares at bay.

It was impossible. When she did drift to sleep, her dreams were of her own death and how the sleazy men would kill her. A variety of ways all pushed forward in her visions. All involved torture and were bloody. She only found comfort in knowing Adam was safe. She might be sacrificed, but he wouldn't be harmed.

The thought brought some relief, but not much. As the hours dragged on, Ella's time grew short. Whatever happened, it would be soon. Her efforts to plot her novel were futile, and the fear of what was to come overwhelmed her. The tortuous night seemed endless, while at the same time she resisted its end, knowing the next day might bring her worst nightmares to life.

The ache in her heart was worse than all of it. Not long before, she'd been in Adam's arms. After giving their marriage vows, life had been filled with joy. Yet, in a moment of inattentiveness, she'd allowed heaven to be ripped away from her. The loss and the terrible thought that she would never see Adam again—never hold him—left a painful chasm inside.

She'd made a mistake in relaxing alertness in a dangerous environment. There was no way to go back, nothing she could do about that. Sick of being a victim of evil, Ella sat up in bed. She strengthened her resolve to find a way out of this mess. Loving Adam too much to give him up, she focused on the present and what offensive action she could take.

The weather had stayed warm, making her glad there had been no need to use the scratchy blanket. Maybe she could wind it into a long strand to use like a rope with which to strangle her aggressor. Yet immediately she discarded the idea. Each man she'd seen was taller and stronger than she, and there was no hope of overwhelming them in that way.

Searching the room, Ella sought some item she might have overlooked, something forgotten that they didn't see as a weapon. Then the key rattled in the doorknob and it turned. Ella missed a breath wondering what would come next. In the solitude of the room, her mind had begun playing tricks on her, and rationality was fleeting.

A tall man entered; his appearance was much like the others who had served her. He carried a tray laden with food and the coffee pot. It was morning. Trembling, partly from lack of sleep and mostly from anxiety, Ella nodded. No matter how rattled she was, the best thing was to appear brave. At least it would not make her such an easy target.

He placed the tray on the bed. As was the custom, he wore a ski mask. It was old, tattered, and didn't fit him well. When he bent to place the food on the blanket, he stretched to reach the low surface of the bed. A corner of the mask pulled up with his motion, and Ella glimpsed his jaw underneath.

With her heart pounding, she took a deep breath and offered a narrow-lipped smile to the man. It was the best she could fake. If Ella had just seen what she thought she had, it could be important. With effort, she cleared her mind, not wanting him to suspect anything. And slowly she walked over to the bed.

The man stepped back, and without looking at him directly, Ella took in his physical appearance. Now she was even more certain. But right then was not the time to dwell on it. Moving with decisive motions but slowly, so as not to seem overly interested, she pushed the top of the small pot and poured some hot coffee in her cup.

Satisfied, the man began to make his way back to the door. At the same time, the chipped porcelain cup slipped from her grip and the steaming coffee splashed over her cheek. "Quente!" she shrieked—"hot" in Portuguese. When the man turned, he seemed unsure what to do, and just froze.

Ella put the cup back on the tray and grabbed the one napkin to dab at the side of her face. She waved one hand to indicate she was all right and forced a slight smile. Seeing that the incident was abated, the man turned toward the door. He looked back once before he left.

On the bed, Ella sat, alone and stunned. Her cheek stung from the incident. But fortunately, the coffee was always served more warm than hot, so no serious injury had resulted. What to do? How to get word to Adam? She had to think. Inspired by what she knew, Ella was invigorated and fully awake, despite her lack of sleep. The one bright spot was that she knew a call would come soon. It had to. And she would be allowed to speak to Adam, even if just for a minute.

*****

Frustrated out of his mind, Adam didn't even try to sleep. On the patio, partially reclined in a lounge chair, he dozed for a few minutes off and on. He was unable to take his mind off Ella, and felt an emptiness he had never experienced before.

Living alone was nothing new. It had been his lifestyle prior to Ella. But now, having fallen so deeply in love with her and having experienced the joy of her by his side, the quiet void of the house drove him crazy. At least outside he could see the expanse of the sky and the dark surface of the bay.

There was space, and that was better than being closed up in an empty house. All day, there had been no word from either Gustavo or Taiz. Now, the night before the exchange was to take place, Adam felt real fear. The prospect of sitting by and trusting that Lawrence and his team could get his wife back was gloomy.

There had to be something more Adam could do, but he didn't know what it was. He'd done all he could, and now he had to wait. But as the hours drained away, his hope did too. The only call had been from Quinn, letting him know that the account number where the funds were to be transferred had been texted. The team leader had acknowledged its receipt and gone back to waiting.

Before dawn, Adam went inside to shower and change. His loyal bodyguard was already in the kitchen drinking coffee. Nico had stayed close throughout the ordeal and intended to go with him to the final negotiations. Neither knew how to defeat Claudio, or how to find Ella, but both would be ready for whatever happened.

As the sky turned orange with sunrise, Nico drove his client back to the law office. Adam sat silently, looking out at the city, seeing little. The ride was short, and once in the conference room, they learned they weren't the first to arrive.

"Lawrence was here before dawn," Quinn told him.

Adam just nodded and began slowly pacing the room. Nico poured more coffee, and the members of the negotiations team sipped theirs, appearing interested in their notes. But there was nothing to prepare. No more was known than nearly forty-eight hours earlier. Only Lawrence looked relaxed, well slept, and confident.

Breaking the silence, two of the team members began discussing some details in low voices. Lawrence went down the hall to use the facilities. And Adam continued to pace. He hated waiting.

Ella was probably waiting too. Only she didn't know what was happening. That would be even worse. And it would be more frightening. Adam's heart hurt, and his agony magnified as he thought of his wife held under such conditions.

Lawrence returned and sat, then leaned back in his chair. The cell phone was on the table in front of him and had been silent since the one text the day before. There was no chance the crooks wouldn't call. Too much money was at stake. The question was: when would they call?

The windows were barely glowing with the rising sun when the cell phone rang sharply. Each man was immediately at attention. Lawrence picked it up and began speaking to the caller. He was the one making the demands, and before anything went further, the caller was ordered to put Ella on the line.

Adam hovered close, and when Lawrence handed him the phone, his hand shook slightly. With his heart pounding, he spoke. "Ella?"

*****

Hearing Adam's voice, she felt a surge of hope. He was there and Ella was talking to him. The blackness of her situation didn't seem quite as bad for a moment. Then the direness of the predicament swamped her. The man who had served her coffee that very morning handed her the phone and Ella knew she had to make every word count. In a flash, he would yank it back.

"Adam, oh God, it's so good to hear you."

"Yes, for me too. Ella, I want to ask you a question, something only you will know." Adam hesitated only for a second. "If I were to buy a complete wardrobe of something you love to see me wear, what would it be?"

Instantly, Ella said, "That's easy. Tuxedos." Then she smiled, for the first time since captivity.

She heard Adam's deep breath, knowing he was relieved.

"It's really you, amore mia. Are you okay? Have they hurt you?"

This was it. Ella's chance. Casually, as if it was just the normal course of conversation, she said, "I am okay. They have not hurt me. Except the hot coffee gave me a burn to the side of my face. I might be disfigured." Then she gave a little laugh as if joking.

The man who had witnessed her spill the coffee glared at her, but she didn't think he spoke English. He grabbed the phone back, and Ella was afraid. Now that the call was over, the ransom would be sent. Then what? Her heart pounded. She hoped Adam would take note of what she'd said, and wouldn't just think she was distraught or not making sense.

The call was over. There were five men, and one of them guided her back to her bedroom while the others talked heatedly. Ella could not understand most of it. But she heard one of them say, "matá-la," and she recognized the Portuguese word for *kill*. Her heart sank. There didn't seem to be any way Adam could get there in time.

*****

Adam looked at his computer screen in disbelief. "The signal is blocked somehow. I'm not able to trace the call."

Quinn shook his head, and Nico sighed deeply.

Then the phone rang for a second time. It was the computerized voice arranging the final trade, and Lawrence handled the conversation like the professional he was. The money would be wired a little later, just inside of the forty-eight-hour deadline. As soon as they received it, they were to call with the details of Ella's location so she could be picked up.

Lawrence put the phone on the table. "That's done. We have until the deadline. Then this will be over. I'll have my team go get Ella. I don't advise you to go, Adam. It's safer if you don't."

Pointing to the computer screen, Adam said, "That second call came from the airport again."

Nico walked over to look. "They are playing with us."

"I'd guess they have men at two different locations," Adam said.

Not long, and it would all be over. Adam's gut told him that the team wouldn't be picking Ella up. Lawrence believed that Claudio and his seedy accomplices would hold up their end of the bargain. But the odds were that they wouldn't.

Adam checked for missed calls on his phone. There was nothing. Gustavo had not called, and it wasn't looking like he would before the deadline. If ever Adam needed to use his cleverness it was then, while he still had a chance. All his life, he'd been outcast for being an oddball prodigy.

Though he'd used his talent to his advantage, it had also attracted the greed of those who wished to profit from it. Right then, Adam was thankful for his intelligence. He didn't have violence or criminal conniving on his side. But he had the brilliance he was born with. And he needed it to come through without delay. Time had run out.

Chapter 19

While Lawrence prepared his team for the final exchange, Adam took his laptop into Quinn's office. Nico followed. It wouldn't take long to set up the wire. He was in no rush to start the transfer of funds.

"I don't know what she meant," Adam said, pacing the room.

"Ella?" His bodyguard stood near the door.

"Yes, when I just spoke to her."

"What did she say, exactly?" Quinn asked.

Adam said, "Her words were 'I am okay. They have not hurt me,' but then she added 'Except the hot coffee gave me a burn to the side of my face. I might be disfigured.'"

Nico stepped closer. "What do you think she meant?"

Adam shook his head. "I've been trying to think. It was a clue. I am sure she was tipping me off."

Quinn drummed a finger on the desk. "Hmm, she's telling you she is okay. But something about the coffee was revealing."

Nico looked lost in thought.

The cell phone in Adam's pocket rang loudly, startling all of them out of their reverie.

"Alô," he said, seeing it was Gustavo. Pacing again, he waited to see what news his friend had, hardly daring to be hopeful.

Gustavo didn't delay telling Adam why he called. It was about Claudio. The words "Ele está morto" were a shock. It couldn't be.

His friend repeated his message "está morto" and went on to relay what details he had. When Adam hung up, he could hardly speak.

Quinn prodded him. "What did he say, Adam?"

Nico watched, missing nothing.

"Claudio is dead."

The silence in the room was deafening. Nobody could believe what they'd just heard.

Nico was the first to speak. "What happened?"

Adam took a breath and repeated what he had just learned. "He died shortly after fleeing to Paraguay. It was a drug overdose."

Quinn frowned. "How does he know that?"

Adam ceased his pacing and looked at his attorney. "Gustavo says he spoke to Juan Ortiz, a man who saw my father when he arrived in Paraguay. They'd done some business together before, and Claudio had nowhere else to stay. Juan allowed him to stay with him for a few days, though he was in a bad way and committed petty crimes to get money for drugs."

Nico stood, drawn in by the new information. "So what happened?"

"Juan was there when it happened. Claudio had gone into the other room and he didn't come out. Looking inside, it was clear he was unconscious. He had no pulse. The syringe was on the table beside his bed. He'd ODed."

Nico and Quinn stared at Adam.

He voiced what they were all wondering. "If Claudio has been dead for over six months, then who kidnapped Ella?"

No one spoke. Adam walked slowly to the chair in front of the desk and sat down to think. Little bits of the puzzle began to piece together.

"I believed it was Claudio as soon as I saw his name

signed to that first threatening letter. But there were things, minor things, that seemed strange."

Quinn gulped some water and sat his glass on the desk. "Like what, Adam?"

"For example, he sent the first text in English. If someone didn't know me like he did, they might think a threat in English would have more impact. I never understood why my father wouldn't just text in Portuguese."

Nico walked over to sit in the chair next to Adam. "What else?"

Adam looked at his bodyguard. "The kidnapping. That's the big thing. My father told Ella, the one time they spoke, that he would never risk having the American government after him. Yet she was abducted, as if he'd changed his mind about that."

Now it was coming together. Adam went on. "And it struck me as odd that Lawrence convinced the crooks my company was in debt, and the ransom money would be hard to get." He looked over at Quinn. "My father knew how I dealt with finances. He would never believe such a lie."

Nico leaned forward and clasped his hands together. "Then we need to figure out who has Ella, and we need to do it fast."

Adam looked past his bodyguard to the clear blue sky as if noticing it for the first time. Ella's words "I might be disfigured" came to mind.

Of course. The burn. "I think I know," he said.

The others waited expectantly.

Adam began to pace again. "It makes so much sense. Who else knew that Claudio tried to extort money from me before, and knew I was wealthy?"

Quinn and Nico looked blank.

Adam smiled. "It was Ella's clue. The burn to the face, the disfigurement."

Suddenly Nico's face showed recognition. "Pietro Cesar!"

"Exactly. When Claudio was coming after us before, Pietro spied on us and Ella saw him. We even got a picture of him."

Then Quinn brightened. "I remember that. I still have the photo you emailed over."

Adam clenched one hand into a fist and smacked it into his other palm. "So that's it. Ella recognized him from the burn on his face. Pietro is her kidnapper."

"Merda," Quinn said.

But Adam was already dialing. Gustavo answered and it didn't take long to enlighten him to what was really going on. The call was short, and the instant he hung up, Adam phoned Taiz.

"It's a go," he said. "We need that team, and we need them fast."

"Where to?"

Adam held his breath. He was so close. This had to work. "I was hoping you could tell me. Claudio is dead. Drug overdose. I'll explain later. The kidnapper is Pietro Cesar."

"The scum of the earth," Taiz said. "Too bad he didn't die in that drug war. But he's scarred forever."

"Yes, and that's how we knew it was him. Ella recognized him. But the reason I am calling you, Taiz, is that I need to know where Pietro hangs out."

"I can help you there. He slinks around in a favela not far from the city. He thinks he is safe there. But I always know where my enemies are."

"Then we need to get going. I'll go with Nico, and we will meet your men there."

Adam handed the phone to his bodyguard, to get the directions for finding the slum where Pietro was holed up.

Quickly, Quinn was filled in on how to handle the funds transfer. "I'll tell Lawrence you control the wire, and everything is set," Adam said, and hesitated at the door with Nico by his side.

Quinn nodded. "I've got it. I'll do exactly as you directed. Get going."

*****

At the perimeter of the property, Adam and Nico spotted a group of men milling about like favela residents. But one wore a blue scarf, as Taiz had said he would, and he casually strolled over to them when they arrived. The operation was filled with risk. The wire would go through anytime, and there was no telling how long after that they'd act against Ella.

If the crooks got the idea that their cover had been blown, they might kill her without a second thought. Taiz had sent Giuseppe, one of his trusted lieutenants, and six armed men. They had no idea how many were inside the slum property. Surely they had them outnumbered.

On the way over, Nico had detailed the plan to Adam. The muscled bodyguard was trained for combat. Adam was not. While the group of soldiers rushed the place and secured the criminals, Nico would follow Adam to keep him safe. They would find Ella and get her out during the attack.

It had all sounded logical when Nico outlined it. But looking at the dilapidated structure, having no idea how many men were inside, Adam felt his stomach flip-flop. He was afraid for Ella. Everything would happen so fast. One of the bad guys could grab her and escape before Adam could get to her. Or a stray bullet could kill her—if a kidnapper didn't kill her first.

But what choice did he have? Seeing the poverty, the neighborhood thick with crime, and knowing Pietro's ruthless nature, Adam knew Ella would not be released as promised. He wouldn't chance it anyway. He had to do everything he could to save her.

There was even a possibility the residence was empty. There hadn't been time to do reconnaissance to verify that Pietro was there, or that Ella was on site. But a sleazy criminal with few resources could hardly afford a hotel room. And where else would he take her? She had to be there.

Adam glanced at his watch then looked at Nico. They'd come straight over but might not be in time. The wire had already gone, and Ella's safety was seriously in question. He nodded at Giuseppe, who flagged his men, and like a well-oiled machine they moved swiftly, half toward the back door and the rest toward the front door. Adam and Nico followed the group to the back.

****

Since Ella had spoken to Adam, she'd listened at her door but couldn't tell what they were saying downstairs. Their voices were just a rumble. She figured the money would arrive soon—either delivered somewhere they'd agreed upon or wired. Either way, it would all be over shortly.

Gently, she'd worked the one slender drawer out of the nightstand. The wood was partly rotted, but it would have to do. The front panel looked sturdy and had a metal knob. With her arms around her only weapon, Ella stood to the side of the door so she would be out of sight when it opened. As she knew it would.

She wasn't sure if she had any chance of survival. But Ella intended to fight. They wouldn't take her easily, as she knew without a doubt that if they took her this time she wouldn't be coming back. Her heart pounded in her chest. And she waited, thinking of Adam. Hoping she would see him again.

Then there were repeated pops that sounded like gunfire. Adrenaline pumped through Ella's slender body and she felt like she could wrestle a grown man to the ground with her bare hands. They weren't going to get her.

Loud noise boomed. There was shouting and more gunshots. Then heavy footsteps thudded on the wooden stairs, headed up toward her room. They were coming. Ella lifted the drawer over her head and watched the knob jiggle. Then it opened.

One of the men from downstairs stepped inside, this time without a mask. In a split second, he realized she

148

wasn't on the bed and he scanned the room for her. With all her might, Ella smacked the drawer down on his head, the hard front panel hitting him hard. The drawer splintered apart and the man staggered but didn't fall.

Ella thought to run, to escape, but before she could move, the man grabbed for her. In the same instant, another man leapt at him, throwing him to the ground. It was Nico. Ella gasped.

As Nico flew by her, Adam raced into the room and pressed Ella against the wall, protecting her with his own body. Across the floor, she could see Nico had the man in a choke hold, with a knife to his throat. "Acabou," he said, breathing heavily. *It's over.* The man didn't move.

As quickly as it had started, it ended. The gunshots ceased and talking could be heard downstairs. Adam held her in a tight embrace while tears streamed down her cheeks. He'd come for her. She was okay. She wasn't going to die.

"Oh my God, Adam," she said, hugging him so tight she was sure he couldn't breathe.

"Ella, Ella," he said. "You're okay. It's going to be all right."

Nico pushed the criminal out of the room, and Ella looked into Adam's eyes.

"I was so scared." Now that it was over, she could admit it. Her muscles felt like jelly and she was lightheaded.

"I know, amore mia. I know." And he hugged her again, like he was afraid to let her go.

Adam's strong body against hers was such a good feeling. She felt safe and so relieved. Life seemed sweeter than ever, like she'd been given a second chance.

"Let's get you out of here," Adam said, and with his arm around her, he guided her out of the tiny room, downstairs and through the back door, into the fresh air. It smelled so good. And it felt wonderful to be outside, to be free again. And to be with Adam. Especially to be with Adam.

Chapter 20

Ella buried her face against Adam's chest, and he wrapped his strong arms around her. She stayed like that for several minutes, hardly able to conceive of what they'd just gone through. When she looked up, Nico was standing quietly, giving them that moment together.

"Giuseppe has everything under control. I think we should go," he said to Adam.

With his arm around his wife to guide her, Adam followed Nico to the car. They slid into the back seat together, and their bodyguard began winding down the hill toward the city. Ella didn't look back.

Adam held her against him, and Ella began to relax. He dialed his phone and said, "Quinn. I have Ella. She is okay. Let Lawrence know it's over. And...proceed as we planned."

Ella was too drained to ask any questions, and trusted that her husband would deal with everything. She placed her palm on his muscled chest, feeling his strength and knowing she was safe. Once they were at home, Nico left too, now that the trauma was over. Other guards stayed on duty, guarding the beach house.

Before the trusted bodyguard exited, Adam shook his hand. "Good job, Nico. I can't thank you enough."

Nico didn't get any words out because Ella wrapped her arms around him. The hug was welcome though unexpected, and he embraced her. "I am glad you are okay, Ella," he said. "You gave us a scare."

With a little laugh, Ella pulled back. "I was more afraid than you were."

"No arguments." Nico smiled and, with a friendly salute, departed.

Ella ran her hands through her stringy hair and sighed. "I'm disgusting. I have to shower."

"Don't be long. You've been away from me more than I can stand."

Ella went into the master bedroom and stripped off her clothes, tossing them in the garbage. She'd never wear them again, no matter how many times they were washed. Bad memories. As she stood under the hot water, her tight muscles began to unwind and her breathing returned to normal.

It had been a rough few days, and the shock would take a while to wear off. But the fear was gone. She was home at last, with Adam. They'd survived the ordeal and were together again. And they had the future. Thinking of that made her happy.

While Ella washed away the scent of her captivity, Adam waited. Smelling of shampoo and dressed in white shorts with a blue cotton shirt, she went out to the pool. He looked up and smiled. He pulled her onto his lap and kissed her tenderly.

"You sure you are okay?" He looked worried.

Ella ran a fingertip over the crease in his brow. "They didn't hurt me. It was terrifying and degrading, but nothing I can't recover from."

He kissed her again, this time rubbing his tongue next to hers. It felt so good to taste him again.

"Let's go down to the beach," he said.

It was still afternoon, and the sun radiated over the white sand, the rays seeping into Ella's bones. She looked out at the bay, loving the ocean, remembering how visions of its beauty had helped her through some of the roughest parts the last few days.

She took a deep breath, then another. "It feels so good just to be by the water, feel the warm day."

They sat down at the beach and Adam held her hand in his. "I don't know what I would have done if anything had happened to you."

Ella lifted his hand in hers and kissed his knuckles. "I wish I hadn't put you through all of that." Then she giggled. "I wish I hadn't put *me* through all of that."

Adam laughed. "That's the truth."

Ella put her head in his lap and he stroked her hair. She watched the waves lap lazily against the shore and dug her toes into the warm sand. It had been traumatic, but she was back where she belonged. And she was with her husband. She loved him so much.

As if reading her mind, Adam said, "I love you, amore mia. With all my heart."

She smiled. "I love you more than I could ever tell you."

Silently, they watched the blue water and soaked up the sun until it began to dim in the sky. Ella fell back in the soft sand and looked up at the sky. Leaning over her, Adam ran his fingertips along her jaw, then kissed her long and lovingly.

"Are you hungry?" he asked, studying her.

"Starved. And I won't be able to eat meat and potatoes for a long, long time."

Adam laughed. "We'll strike it from the menu."

Taking his hand, Ella let him pull her up, and they embraced. Standing with the water lapping their toes, they clung together, thankful to have each other. Adam kissed the top of her head.

"Let's go, then. Eli should be here by now. He will have some amazing feast for us, I'm sure."

They jogged hand in hand back to the patio and saw the table covered with a white cloth and decorated with gold candles.

Adam glanced at Ella. "Looks like he is expecting us."

She stepped closer to the lovely table. "I'll say. I'll be spoiled again in no time."

Pulling out her chair, Adam said, "I plan on spoiling you from now on."

Knowing her tastes, Eli served white fish tacos with avocado, the fish grilled to perfection. One half of the plate was filled with fresh salad tossed in cilantro dressing. To accompany the special meal, Adam requested champagne, a Krug Grande Cuvee.

They lifted their glasses and clinked to toast. "To being together," Adam said.

Ella grinned. "To fresh food and showers."

Adam laughed. During the meal, he seemed hardly able to take his eyes off of her. Ella periodically rubbed her bare toes against his foot, feeling the electricity radiate through her. They ate and drank, life's joy slowly restoring.

As they worked their way through the bottle of champagne, Ella felt deliciously lightheaded. The heavy burden she'd endured for days faded away, and she leaned back in her chair. Her handsome husband looked a little tired, but it did nothing to detract from his sex appeal. A warm tingle grazed her skin when she let her eyes linger over his lean, sculpted form.

Adam reached in his pocket and pulled out a small gold band. "That last morning, you left this on the dresser."

Ella remembered getting ready and rushing out to meet Kaiyla. "Well, that's one thing they didn't steal."

After slipping it on her left finger, Adam lifted her hand to kiss the ring. "My wife, my beautiful, amazing wife," he said.

Her heart swelled with love and she leaned forward to accept the warm kiss he gave her, feeling so adored. And even feeling beautiful. That was how Adam always made her feel.

A stunning orange sunset flamed in the sky just as Eli served dessert—hazelnut affogato. It was a creamy Italian-inspired treat, made by pouring hot espresso over vanilla ice cream and adding hazelnut syrup. The dish was one of Ella's favorites, and though their chef had no idea what she'd been through the past few days, he did know she'd been away. Making the dreamy dessert was his way of saying "welcome home."

The dessert was served in a porcelain cup, and around the edge of the saucer were a few roasted coffee beans. The lovely presentation inspired Ella and, taking a scoop of the exquisite concoction, she fed it to Adam.

Grinning, he let the creamy bite melt in his mouth. Then Adam scooped some and fed Ella. Both remembered a time when they had made love in the kitchen, over dessert—literally. Neither needed to say anything, but each bite teased and tantalized.

If Ella hadn't been so wiped out, she might have attacked Adam on the spot. But the dearth of sleep and the recent stress caught up to her. Tranquilized by the champagne and satisfied by the gourmet meal, her eyes began to close, despite her best effort at staying awake.

But she didn't want to go inside. For too many hours, Ella had been locked in a small space, unable to feel the sun or even breathe the air. Maybe later she would be able to go in and rest on her soft bed, but not right away.

Eli cleared the table and took his leave. Adam lowered the back of one of the lounge chairs and opened his arms for Ella to join him. She nestled between his legs with her head on his chest. Gazing up at a night sky illuminated by city lights, she fell instantly asleep.

*****

When Ella woke up, she was in her own bed, but had no memory of how she got there. Morning light brightened the windows, and she snuggled against her pillow, wanting a few more minutes in her cozy bed. Recalling the romantic dinner with Adam, she smiled.

He was so gorgeous and so caring. She was lucky, and she knew it. Yawning and stretching, Ella came to life. The thought of another warm shower inspired her to get up.

Though she could smell the aroma of Brazilian coffee wafting through the air, she went straight to the bathroom.

Before going out to see Adam, she retrieved her diamond engagement ring from the drawer and slipped it on her finger next to the gold band. It was so beautiful. Wearing a soft floral skirt, a sleeveless blouse, and low-heeled sandals, Ella went down the hall to find Adam.

As she rounded the corner, she saw him at the kitchen table talking on the phone. After pouring a steaming cup of coffee, she sat next to him. He smiled at her and mouthed the word *Taiz*.

Ella nodded, and Adam pushed a button, switching his phone to speaker. "I have Ella with me."

"Ah, Ella. You have had a couple of very exciting days."

She laughed. "A little too exciting."

"Well, I was just asking your husband to resolve a mystery for me."

"What's that?" Ella asked.

"It's very odd. The ransom was wired to the crooks, but then it vanished."

Ella looked up at Adam and he shrugged, but his eyes twinkled.

"So, Adam. Would you care to fill me in?"

"I will gladly tell you. After all, you had my back during a very bad time."

Taiz's deep chuckle vibrated through the cell phone speaker. "You owe me."

"A lot," Adam said. "I had Quinn wire the funds using some banking software I developed."

"Is it like disappearing ink?"

Ella smiled at the question.

"Sort of." Adam grinned. "I programmed it. I made it appear that the funds were there, but they never really transferred. Once we knew Ella was safe, Quinn had instructions to hit a button, later that day; it would make the screen change. Magically, it then showed the reality. There was no money there."

"You fooled them, Adam. You are brilliant. So you have the money in your possession, and Ella, too. Clever."

"Well, I don't really have the money," Adam said, still smiling.

"And why not?" Taiz asked.

"I've donated it to Gustavo's foundation."

Taiz laughed again. "I would say it's poetic justice that the same funds the criminals sought to extort from you will now help with much-needed reform."

Adam grinned. "I thought so."

"You've made my day. Remind me to arrange a meeting soon. I'm interested to see what new software I can purchase from you. Your talent has already led to profits for me."

"The gambling software?"

"It's been very lucrative."

"Okay then, we will meet soon."

The call ended and Ella stared at Adam. "So they stole the money, and you stole it back."

"Let's say they *thought* they stole the money."

She giggled. "Amazing."

Adam stood and pulled his wife into his arms. "How about breakfast out? I'm tired of being cooped up in here."

It sure sounded good to Ella. "Let me grab my purse."

Breakfast was near the beach at Confeitaria Colombo, famous for pastries since the late 1800s. It had a postcard view of Copacabana Beach and an extensive menu. At an outside table, Ella sipped her steaming coffee and admired the view of the ocean.

The beach and the surf had been Ella's therapy over the years. Locking her away in a windowless room had more of a penalty than her captors had known. She ordered a waffle with blackberry jam; Adam's waffle came with ham and cheese. They split a thick milkshake made with vanilla ice cream, yogurt, and guava. Too full after the waffles, they couldn't finish it.

It was another beautiful day in Rio, and since the coffee shop was located at Copacabana Fort, they decided to tour it. They had a view of the entire stretch of the beach, and Sugarloaf in the distance. After strolling along the promenade, they found a shady place to sit at the end of the rocky point.

Adam held her hand and gazed at her rings. Touching the sparkling diamond with his finger, he smiled. "You're so beautiful, Ella."

The way he said it moved her deeply, and for a moment she was speechless.

He looked out at the expansive view, to the endless ocean and the blue sky above. Turning to look at her, Adam said, "There's something you should know."

Ella raised her eyebrows.

"My father is dead."

The evening before, they hadn't discussed the kidnapping and Ella had been glad. She wanted to put it behind her and just recover. But this was important.

"What happened? How did you find out?"

Adam took a breath and began telling her the story, everything she'd missed. He explained how he'd learned that Claudio had not survived for long in Paraguay.

"I can't say I'm sorry to hear that," Ella said. "How did you take the news?"

Adam looked thoughtful. "I was relieved. The man made my life miserable from the moment I drew my first breath. And he never changed his ways. It affected you, too. And that I could not tolerate." He looked at her. "I'm glad he's gone."

"One enemy gone."

"Actually two," Adam said.

"Who is the other?"

"This morning, before you came into the kitchen, Taiz had just finished telling me that Pietro Cesar would never bother us again. Though if things had not worked out as they had, he would have killed you as we feared."

Ella squeezed her husband's hand. "What did he say?"

"Giuseppe, the man who led us against the kidnappers, learned that Pietro left the favela right after they let you speak to me on the phone. I'm guessing that's when he went to meet his real partner in the kidnapping, leaving the other four crooks behind. We traced two of the calls to the airport, so it would make sense that Pietro's partner was already there, having placed the final call for the ransom right after I spoke to you."

Ella waited.

Taking a moment, Adam looked into the distance as if deciding how to proceed. "My deceit with the banking software resulted in his demise." He looked back at Ella and went on. "The four that held you captive were to be paid a nominal fee, just for being your jailers. They had no idea what the ransom amount was, nor did Taiz see the need to enlighten them.

"But Pietro had the other partner that he had promised to share the wealth with. When they verified the funds transfer on their computer, both were happy. But when the funds disappeared, Pietro tried to explain that it was a trick. His partner, expecting to get rich from their scheme, didn't believe him. They fought. Convinced he had been betrayed, and unable to wring the truth from Pietro...he killed him."

Nothing was said for a few minutes.

Ella spoke first. "So we have no living enemies."

"No, amore mia. Our enemies are gone."

Chapter 21

Ella could tell Adam didn't want to go home. He told her he'd been torn apart from his wife for too many days, and intended to remedy their injured hearts, both his and Ella's.

"I'm taking you somewhere special," he said.

Miguel drove them to a boutique hotel in the rain forest near Corcovado, a place called Largo do Boticário. The guest house was a mansion from the mid-1800s and had only two suites. Adam wanted privacy, and so rented both of them.

The hand-painted Portuguese tiles, baroque roof carved in wood, and a staircase in marble and iron taken from an Italian palace were like something out of a storybook. Large painted murals on the walls told the house's history.

Though Adam's team followed and maintained a secure perimeter, Ella barely noticed. She would never again resent having bodyguards. They were a part of living in Rio, and even more, a part of being wealthy. It was a small price to pay for being with the man she loved.

The home was secluded on one of Rio's quaintest cul-de-sacs, and Ella was transported both physically and emotionally. The suite was stylish. On the polished wood floor was one bed covered with a thick quilt, under a sheer partial canopy. It was inviting and intimate. Gold fabric pillows were piled at the top.

Ella turned to look at Adam. His amber eyes were filled with lust.

"I crave you," he said, and pulled her into his arms. He kissed her hotly and nipped at her lower lip. Then he released her and began unbuttoning her blouse.

"I want to see you naked, amore mia. I want to have you."

Melting at his words, Ella let him remove her blouse and then her skirt. She kicked off her sandals and felt the cool wood under her feet.

Wanting Adam as much as he wanted her, Ella pulled his shirt off over his head and drank in the sight of his bare chest. "I need you, Adam," she whispered.

It had been too long since she'd been alone with her sexy husband. For days, she'd thought she might never see him again. And as horrible as that was, now that he was so near, it made being with him all the more precious.

She removed her bra and panties while Adam shoved down his pants and shorts. Then he scooped her up and carried her to the bed.

As she looked at his tousled golden hair, his handsome face, and soft lips, desire swamped her.

"I thought I'd lost you," she said.

"Never." Adam looked into her eyes, his gaze piercing into her. "You will never lose me."

As he began making love to her, slowly and patiently, Ella was lost in his sensuality. She'd never known a man could be like Adam. The mere sight of him made her swoon. To add to the effect he had on her, the way he cared for her and understood was beyond what she could have ever hoped for.

Not only did her need for him evaporate any control, but the emotional strength she found in his arms spiraled her to the heights of ecstasy. At first, Adam played with her lovingly. He caressed her bare breasts and licked and sucked her aching nipples.

Then he fondled her sex, running his finger across her

wet slit, teasing her. Ella became more and more aroused. She whimpered and moaned, unable to hold all the feeling inside. With expert touching, Adam took her close to orgasm, only to back away.

"You are driving me crazy," she gasped.

"It's what you deserve," he whispered. "You drive me crazy all the time."

Again and again, he fingered her tight clit but never gave her quite enough. At the point where she prayed he would take her to full release, Adam backed off. Instead, he kissed her all over. He found every sensitive area and pressed his lips to her skin.

Ella tingled with delight and fisted his thick cock. It was hot and heavy in her hand, turning her on even more. Pre-cum seeped from the tip, and she knew Adam was as close as she was to losing it. She cupped his balls and rolled them in her hand, loving his moan.

The teasing gave way to passion, and Adam no longer held back. He wanted her and made no secret of it. His kisses were harder and hotter. Ella raked her tongue around the inside of his mouth, tasting his male flavor.

He cupped her ass, squeezing possessively, and her sex throbbed. Needing him inside her, Ella pressed her belly against his hard shaft, panting to keep her need at bay. There was no reason to wait, no reason to be apart.

Ella was on her side, facing Adam. He slipped two fingers inside her and massaged her gently, then withdrew. He grabbed the base of his erection and slid into her, just a little, and she gasped. It felt too good. She pressed down on him, taking more.

"Adam...I need you inside me."

With ferocity, he plunged his length deeply into her, and Ella panted louder as did Adam. On her side, he filled her up, but it felt different, tighter. She rubbed against him, getting friction on her needy clit.

Adam held her tight, with his palm on her ass, and she pressed her sex against him. They rocked back and forth, stroking. Each motion brushed her clit, pushing her closer to the edge. The tips of her nipples grazed him; she could feel the light hair on his chest tickle her in the most delicious way.

Time was of no significance. Alone in the quiet of the old mansion, the only sound was their own moans. Adam fucked her with abandon. His skin gleamed with the effort, and Ella wanted to come badly, but held off, wanting the moment to last forever.

As they moved together, sensations intensifying, and Ella's sex clenching deep in her core, they exploded. All at once, Adam groaned in a low, primal voice, and Ella felt a bolt of heat sear through her. She screamed in a high-pitched cry.

His cock pulsed powerfully within her and Ella convulsed around it. The release bound them together, sealing them off in a universe of their own. Something no one else could know or share. Something that melded them into one.

Adam came long and hard as Ella was propelled to a higher plane. Her entire body warmed and then relaxed, with a heavy sensation of pleasure settling inside her and showing no sign of leaving. Adam closed his eyes for a moment and Ella kissed his bare chest.

He rolled on his back, taking her with him. On top, she looked down at the man she loved with all her heart. Adam raised his head to kiss her then brushed her hair back from her cheek. "I'm not done," he whispered.

"Nor am I." Ella covered her mouth with his, kissing him, drinking him in. She could never get enough. She would never be able to get enough.

Undisturbed, secluded in the colonial mansion, Adam made love to her again and again. He was insatiable, as was she. It was a dream, a wonderful, sexy dream. There was nothing to separate them, nothing to threaten their peace. And there never would be again.

Through the night, they loved each other, taking breaks to nap—but only to awaken again, with the fire of desire burning hot. At last, as dawn peeked into the sky, Ella fell asleep in Adam's arms, happier than she'd ever been.

*****

They stayed for three more days in the romantic suite, venturing out for food to sustain their energy and to soak in more of the Brazilian sun. When they did return home, it was with some reluctance. But immediately they started looking forward to their honeymoon and more time in each other's arms.

Adam worked when he could, and Ella began to outline her next novel. They surfed together most mornings. Eli cooked and Nico watched over them. Life was as it should be. It wasn't often that Ella wrote in her diary anymore. But shortly after the getaway to the secluded mansion, she felt compelled to make a much-needed entry.

I used to say my life was boring, and I felt plain. Now I can't imagine feeling that way. The day Adam appeared, he lit up my life and it has never been the same. It never will. I'm deeply, madly, crazy in love with him. He's the man I crave, and the man I want to spend my life with.

The best part is that he loves me too, as much as I love him. And he tells me all the time how beautiful I am. We had to fight to protect what we have. It hasn't been easy. But we never had any doubt about each other. That was never the problem.

Now we don't have to fear our enemies. Their own bad conduct led ultimately to their demise. I can't say I wish that on anyone. But I have to admit, I feel no sadness about it either. They are gone, and we can finally be happy.

*****

Adam decided it was best not to tell the family what had happened, and Ella agreed. When Fiorella returned from her honeymoon, she moved in with Adrian. She looked radiant, and if she noticed any difference in Adam or Ella, she probably assigned it to their newlywed condition.

There was one thing Adam needed to tell her, and that was about her father's death. She was immensely relieved, and could hardly believe that Claudio would never trouble them again. Together they told Serena, who had a similar reaction.

Kaiyla and Steve were never the wiser. As far as they knew, they'd flown back to Newport with Ella in her husband's arms. Even if Ella had told her, it was a fantastic story, and hard to conceive that it had really happened. It was better to let her friend believe her own version.

Gustavo was pleased to receive the sizable donation to his foundation, and surprised at his new converts. Apparently, wanting to stay on the right side of the law, Taiz had instructed his men to shoot only if needed. At the scene of the rescue, they had used gunfire to scare the kidnappers, but, finding them unarmed had no need to injure.

However, the pressure was on, and Taiz threatened the four men left behind. "Either get into one of Gustavo's programs and reform, or I'll make your life not worth living." Though he was a respectable businessman by then, Taiz remained intimidating. And the scraggly crew had no doubt he would follow through with his threat. Whether or not they reformed, Ella didn't know. But they did enter the program.

Best of all, the honeymoon finally arrived. There was one place Ella had always wanted to go. All the years she had surfed in Newport Beach, and later Rio, she had dreamed of going to Hawaii. In the fall, the swells were starting to get bigger but the crowds were sparse—the best conditions for surfing. The visiting pros hadn't arrived since the winter season wasn't in full swing, so the beaches weren't packed yet.

The JW Marriott Ihilani Resort and Spa was as luxurious as it boasted in the brochures. Set on a private beach cove with breathtaking views, it was the ideal hotel for a honeymoon. Surfing on the beaches of Oahu was a dream come true, second only to being Adam's wife.

The mornings were for surfing, and the nights for passionate lovemaking, with the afternoons falling into either category as they saw fit. Early one day, just after dawn, they paddled into the surf. Looking in her direction, Ella's gorgeously-tanned husband smiled.

"Ready?" Adam said.

"Yes," Ella called, just as they reached the beginning of a swell. The giant aqua-blue wave swept them up in unison, and together they carved a path down the inside of the curl. The sun was warm, and the fresh ocean air whipped against her face.

The exhilaration of riding the wave was magnified by having Adam with her. Side by side, they raced toward the shore. Ella was reminded of the first day they met, not so long before, when she'd slid down a powerful wave, right into the arms of the man she would forever crave.

PERFECTLY FLAWED

NEW ADULT ROMANCE

By

Emily Jane Trent

Chapter 1

Numb and uninterested in baseball, Adrianna pulled the cuff of her long-sleeved shirt down, rubbing her wrist. Meeting someone, or falling in love, was low on her list of priorities, so she certainly didn't come to the game to meet some cool guys from the other school like her friends did. Regretting her decision to tag along, Adrianna wished she were anywhere else but in a dusty sports field. One more month until graduation and she'd be free of her parents, and that was her goal in life, at least as far as she could see.

As she scuffled along in the dirt, heading toward the snack bar for a Coke, her powder-blue tennis shoe caught on a rock and she nearly lost her balance. Distracted, she hardly noticed those around her. It was warm and sunny, the opposite of her mood. And it was crowded, which she found annoying. Why she let her friends talk her into coming she wasn't sure.

A voice pierced her reverie, the male tone mocking her, the words slurring. "Hey, baby."

She'd heard it many times before. It was best to ignore leering men; that much she'd learned. Lowering her head and letting her wispy blond hair fall over her eyes, Adrianna increased her gait. Hoping to get past the offensive male attention, she clutched the front of her shirt, trying to be invisible.

The male form she plowed into reeked of alcohol and smelled of cigarette smoke and body odor. Instinctively, she veered around the offender, causing her to stumble; her butt hit the dirt before she could react. Rough hands lifted her, making her cringe. *Don't touch me.*

The male was drunk and scruffy; his eyes were glazed over. "Well, look what I found," he said with an ugly grin. Two others, dressed similarly in faded jeans and dirty cotton shirts with some gaudy design on the front, hacked in laughter.

No one seemed to be paying attention to them. Adrianna wrestled against the black-haired guy's grip, which he found amusing. "Are you lost, love? You are a beauty, aren't you?" He taunted in a garbled swirl of words, making her skin crawl.

Nausea hit her stomach, but refusing to give in, she struggled harder. To no avail. His two friends moved closer, surrounding her. Desperate, she kicked her attacker in the shin, but all he did was jump back, laughing. "Let me go," she ordered, and kicked him again, with little effect. He was probably too soused to feel pain.

"Oh, you are a feisty one." Her captor leered at her.

"Not quite as feisty as I am," a deep male voice boomed. Whoever it was stood close by, but Adrianna couldn't see him at first, with her view blocked by the three that had her trapped. The voice had a lilt—Irish, she guessed. It was subtle but there.

The three didn't react at first, just stood firm. Surrounded, Adrianna choked at the stench. Clearly, bathing was not high on their list of priorities. The dark-haired one relaxed his grip on her slightly, but did not let go.

"I think you've made a mistake," the voice said with confidence. The bold accusation held threat, subdued but ready to explode if the owner of that magnificent voice were provoked.

"I don't think so, buddy," the aggressor spat, the smell

of alcohol on his breath enough to make Adrianna reel. "Mind your own business."

"Step back." The words were spoken harshly and definitively. It was clearly a warning.

The two others stepped away, leaving the one attacker alone with her. His face was rigid but his eyes showed uncertainty.

And Adrianna could understand why. Now that the view was unblocked, she could see where the voice came from, and for a moment forgot about her own plight. Before her stood a heartthrob if there ever was one. Her breath caught in her throat and weakness seeped into her muscles.

He stood at least six feet and was all muscle, built larger than most of the boys she knew in her high school. His short-cropped brown hair was buzzed close on the sides, the top a bit longer, gelled and spiked. In a white fitted T-shirt stretched across his well-developed pectorals, and tight blue jeans accenting his sculpted thighs, he was a sight to behold.

But it was his eyes that drew her to him. They were a rich caramel color, deep and intense. Glaring, he challenged anyone to argue with him, and none dared. Yet, at the same time, Adrianna could feel him looking at her in his peripheral vision like he saw everything, taking in the entire scene at once.

"I don't think you want me to tell you again," he said. "Step back, and be on your way."

The dark-haired weasel hesitated. His eyes darted from his friends to the tall challenger and back again. Seeing them stepping back farther, he dropped his hands. "Whatdaya think? I was just helping the lady. She tripped."

The caramel eyes never wavered, the look searing into the coward before him. The loser ran his hands through his greasy hair and took a step back. His eyes roamed up and down all six feet of Adrianna's sturdy rescuer. He held up both hands, palms flat to protect against any approach, in an "I don't want to fight" gesture.

Then he slid away, leaving Adrianna alone with her new friend—as "friend" he'd proven to be very quickly. Shyness took over and she hugged herself, still a little rattled from the experience, and nervous in the presence of one so gorgeous.

Awed, she looked down at the dirt now dusted over the power-blue canvas of her shoes, turning them softly brown. The silence pulled her attention back to the moment. Looking up and risking a glance into the caramel eyes, she noted a hint of a smile on his face.

"Are you okay?"

"I guess so," she replied, thinking what a lame answer that was. Of course, she wasn't okay. She was never okay, not before she was attacked, and most certainly not after. "Thank you for scaring them off."

"Didn't take much to scare them."

Adrianna gazed at him. Not much? Did he have any idea what an imposing stature he possessed? "Well, you came just in time. I'm not sure what he had in mind, but it wouldn't have been pleasant."

"Definitely not pleasant." There was that hint of a smile again. "I'm Sean Reid." He held out a strong hand politely.

"I'm Adrianna Brooks." She touched his hand and felt the electricity. The feeling rattled her, making her legs a little shaky. "I better get back to my friends." The comment was offered more as an escape than anything else. Halfway hoping he'd talk her out of parting, Adrianna didn't make a move to leave.

He nodded, and for a minute, like he was going to say something else. But he didn't.

"Okay then," she said, and took a step away.

The Coke long forgotten, Adrianna walked slowly back in the direction of her friends. Each step was like molasses. All she wanted was for him to call after her, stop her, tell her... Tell her what? This was crazy. She'd just met this guy. What in the world could he tell her?

That everything would be okay? That he wanted to see

her again? And again and again? Because Adrianna didn't want to leave. Being near him felt...different, in an unfamiliar way. It felt safe. And it felt good. Both were foreign to her, and she wasn't sure she liked it. The feeling threw her off, unnerved her.

But the pull was strong. Given the least provocation, she would have stayed with him. At least for a bit. At least until she could think this through. But no. Such was not to be. Not for her. That was not her life, not by a long way. He didn't fit. He couldn't fit. Fate had thrown him in her path for some reason, but it clearly wasn't to make things better for her.

*****

Sean watched her walk away. *Those blue eyes.* She was a stunner. The sight of her—softly rounded curves, long blond hair, and designer jeans—was all class. He'd almost asked for her phone number, and he should have. He huffed, expelling a deep breath, kicking himself for letting her go.

Never shy with girls, he couldn't fathom what his problem was. *Get a grip.* But then she wasn't from his school. She couldn't be; he would have noticed her. Definitely. Maybe she was from a private school. That had to be it. No one in his school dressed quite like that, not really. Even he could tell her jeans and shirt were made by some expensive designer.

Yep, out of his class. No question. Then why was he still gawking? The sway of her hips, the delicate way she stepped, like she'd been to some prep school where they teach you how to walk. Good thing he'd been around when he had; he dreaded to think of that slime ball with his hands on her.

He lost sight of her and reluctantly turned to go. His buddies waited in the bleachers. "Where the hell have you been?"

"Can't a guy go to the bathroom?"

The click of the bat on the ball yanked attention back to

the game. The Boston high school crowd roared and his buddies yelled. Sean couldn't have cared less. Nothing against baseball. He'd just found something much more interesting. *Get over it. It's not going to happen.*

"Ahhhh, out, out out," Tomas shouted. His pale green eyes squinted against the sun and he held one hand over his brow to block the glare. Shaggy brown hair brushed his jaw and his honed muscles flexed under his cotton shirt. The game wasn't going how he'd anticipated and his body tensed, fighting against his team losing.

Sean had been friends with him since grade school, forming a strong bond. Baseball was a recent source of interest for his Irish friend. Fighting had held much more allure, as it had for Sean, in the time they'd spent enduring school and prejudice that long since claimed to be gone, but wasn't.

His other pal, Nic, leaned back with both hands on his head, and groaned. "Noooo, come on," he yelled. Niccolo Romano—dark hair, icy blue eyes—was Italian, not Irish, but in some ways that made him even a better ally. The Irish were fierce; throw an Italian in the mix and the combo could be unstoppable. Time and again, Nic had been a good friend to have when the going got tough.

Some would say they were part of a gang. But Sean didn't see it that way. They protected each other, watched each other's back, that was all. It was survival. Fighting was part of life, at least any life Sean had known. And he'd been ready and willing to thump that jerk who had his greasy hands on Adrianna.

But he hadn't needed to. Sometimes the right tone, the look in your eye, stopped the enemy cold. And maybe a good look at Sean's heavily muscled form had something to do with it. Probably it was better he hadn't had to punch the guy. Adrianna might have gotten a bad impression of him. Sometimes women recoiled at fighting, even though fighting was necessary. It was smart to avoid it, if one could. But sometimes it had to be done.

Caring what Adrianna thought was useless. He'd never

see her again. And if he did, the odds were that she would act like she didn't know him. Well, she didn't, not really. But he knew the arrogance of the rich, and no self-respecting girl from a private school would want to be seen associating with a thug like him. He was proud, and respected who he was and his heritage. But that didn't mean she would.

The sun beat down on them, making Sean thirsty. He reached under the seat for his jacket and pulled the flask out of the inside pocket. A swig of whiskey would hit the spot. He'd tried to convert to beer, drinking it most of the time. But it wasn't always convenient, and some occasions called for something stronger.

Meeting Adrianna was one such occasion. She had affected him more than he cared to admit. A pale beauty with her sky-blue eyes and light blond hair, she was a woman that roused powerful feelings inside, but one he was never to have. He knew that. So there was no point in tormenting himself. None at all. He took another swig and twisted the cap back on the flask.

"This game sucks," Nic said.

"It's over anyway. They can't recover," Tomas whined, in pain for his team.

Sean grabbed his jacket and stood.

"Got anything in there worth sharing?" Tomas nodded toward the jacket.

"I might. Let's get to the truck first."

At the bottom of the steps, Sean led them toward the exit. Up ahead, he spotted Adrianna with her girlfriends. Relief that she wasn't with a guy flooded through him. *Stupid. Don't be stupid. She's not yours.*

"Hey, you guys know that girl, the blond one?" Sean pointed toward the back of Adrianna's head, his eyes drifting down her round hips and long legs.

"The beauty queen?" Nic looked over at Sean.

"Shut up. I don't need your snide comments. Just answer. Do you know who she is or not?"

"I know her," Tomas said.

"You do? How do you know her?"

"My sister knows her. They've been to a couple of parties together. She's a looker. I'll give her that. But not your speed, Sean. She's a rich bitch."

Sean glared at Tomas.

"Sorry. Just saying."

"Can you get me her phone number?" Sean didn't avert his gaze from Adrianna, and she must have felt it because she glanced back. Briefly their eyes met, but she instantly looked away.

"What for?" Tomas stopped in the parking lot for a second, unsure which direction they'd parked the truck.

"This way," Sean said, pointing toward his truck. "Because I want to call her."

"Yeah, well, I don't see the purpose. But I'll see if I can get it for you. I'll have to think of some story to tell my sister."

"Well, do it. As a favor to me."

Sean had no idea what had gotten into him. Well, actually, he did. Adrianna was in his blood; the sight of her heated his veins and stirred a flame that would need little fanning to roar to life. He should forget her, forget he met her. But he knew he wouldn't. No chance.

Spotting his faded blue Chevy, he headed in that direction, his buddies on his heels. He was more inclined to turn and race after Adrianna instead of hopping in the truck with his pals. An ache started in his chest and drifted down to his gut. The knowledge that she was going to get in a car and leave was a knife in his chest.

Sean wanted her. And despite the unlikely chance that he would ever have her, plans of what to say when he called were already forming in his mind. With the right approach, it was possible she'd agree to see him. After all, he did save her. That was a good start, something to build on. Having no idea what he would really say when he called, Sean felt bereft, like he'd lost someone that meant a lot to him. Which was true. But he was going to fix that. He was going to see Adrianna again.

175

Chapter 2

From the back seat of the cream-colored Mercedes, Adrianna watched thick green trees roll by. Looking beyond into the expanse of blue sky, she wished the luxury car weren't taking her home. An elusive thought that she might escape flitted through her mind and left before she could consider it seriously.

The soft beige leather seat cushioned her ride, giving her a false sense of comfort. The sedan was a graduation gift. Cari Harper had been Adrianna's best friend since she could remember. The car had been the Harpers' idea of the proper way to acknowledge their only daughter's graduation. Completely overdone, but generous.

Cari had ash-blond hair and gray-blue eyes. She was pretty and naturally thin, which Adrianna wasn't, much to her detriment. Her mother and Cari's were both affluent; appearance was a high priority. Adrianna wondered if she'd ever be able to live her life without caring about what other people would think. It was so ingrained she had trouble imagining life without it.

But Cari was a good friend, a nice person. She just seemed more acclimated to the high-class lifestyle in Beacon Hill, never complaining and only enjoying the benefits. Having kind, loving parents didn't hurt. Whereas Adrianna's mother carped continually, finding fault with everything about her one and only daughter, Cari's mother showered her with approval.

The other girl that had come with them, Shelby Logan, attended the same private school. And though they weren't as tight, Adrianna liked her well enough. Brunette with hazel eyes, she was pretty enough but never entered any of the contests. She was rail thin, and though attractive in her way, didn't get as many offers for dates. Her lips were overly full, which looked a bit odd on her, and were out of balance with her other features.

Often Adrianna was jealous because Shelby's mother didn't rag on her to change, or pressure her to be different. Adrianna couldn't imagine. Since she was a child, it seemed her mother had forced her into one type of beauty pageant or another. The fact that she developed curves as she entered her mid-teens aggravated her mother.

Hannah Lane Brooks, her annoying mother, had been born into wealth and married wealth. It was all she knew. And showing off her daughter seemed to be her sole career, other than charity luncheons or society parties, if that was what they even called them anymore.

"That was a bust," Shelby said. "All the cute guys were with someone. What a waste. I didn't find anyone to hit on."

Cari turned down the music and said, "Yeah, me either. And the game was boring."

"I met someone," Adrianna blurted out.

"You?" her friends said in unison.

"Why is that so shocking?"

"Because you know you're always the shy one. We didn't see you with anyone. Who did you meet? Who is he?" Cari glanced in the rearview mirror, anxious for details.

"Sean Reid."

"You're kidding." Shelby's mouth fell open.

"No, I'm not kidding. Why? Do you know him?"

"No, well I don't *know* him, not like that. I know *of*

him. And he's not the guy for you."

"How would you know? I liked him."

"For starters, he's Irish."

"Oh, and now you're a bigot."

"No, I am not a bigot. But your parents are...don't act like you don't know what I mean. Your mother would kill you if you were with him."

"Why?"

"Okay, well, I saw him at a party. It was at a friend's house. I'm not even sure what he was doing there. But he's not just Irish, he hangs out with these other guys—tough guys, you know. They have a reputation for fighting. And he doesn't live in our neighborhood."

"Really? So that rules him out...that he doesn't live in our snooty, stuffy neighborhood?"

"Don't be bitter. I'm just saying how your parents would see it. You're supposed to marry a nice Protestant boy."

"Yes, I'm sure. But I'm eighteen; I'm an adult. They can't rule my life. If I want to see the guy, I'll see him. And as soon as I graduate I'm moving out anyway."

Shelby shrugged, and Cari glanced in the rearview mirror again. Miffed, Adrianna looked out the window, distressed to see they were nearly at her house. The Mercedes glided effortlessly up the hill and pulled to the curb. From the street, the brick home didn't look so bad. It was the same architectural style as so many in the area. Surrounded by trees and lawn, it was impressive—if one didn't know what was inside, that is.

"Okay, see you later." Adrianna got out and watched her friends drive off. Delaying the inevitable, she looked around at her neighbors' homes, at least what she could see. The brick buildings with wooden shuttered windows and ironwork spoke of an earlier time. The mansions were as elaborately decorated inside as one would expect. She'd been inside many of them for events she would have rather skipped.

Knowing her mother would likely be home, Adrianna

didn't hurry to go in, dreading the encounter. Reluctantly, she stepped inside and instantly felt claustrophobic. The mint-green walls with white trim gave the main room a cold, formal feel. The room was rarely used, though it had a white wood-framed fireplace, great for cold winters. It was mostly for show.

Everything was for show: the room, the house, their life, and most of all, Adrianna.

Her mother stuck her head around the corner. "I thought I heard you." Like her daughter, she had blond hair and blue eyes. Her perfect bone structure and trim figure were a source of pride. "Why did you wear that shirt? Long sleeves? It's warm today. What were you thinking?"

Adrianna didn't bother to answer; the question didn't deserve an answer. There was always a critical remark as a greeting, and she was used to it. She walked past her mother, going straight to her bedroom to lock the door.

"Adrianna, you're coming out for dinner. You can't stay in that bedroom all the time." The sound of her mother's voice grated her nerves and was a source of depression. Again, she didn't answer. It wasn't expected.

Flopping on her bed, Adrianna breathed in the odor of furniture polish and disinfectant. The maid must have cleaned. *When I have my own place I'm never going to clean*, she thought. She bent her knees, putting her dusty shoes on the pure white quilt. Her mother would have a fit if she saw her. An advantage to having a lock on her door. Staring up at the ornate edging separating the stark white ceiling from the sunny yellow walls, Adrianna tried to imagine she was somewhere else.

She grabbed her iPod from the drawer, and blocking out all other sound with her earphones, she cranked up the music, letting Death Cab for Cutie belt out "You Are A Tourist" to drown out anything her mother might shout from the hallway. Music was an escape, a necessity, the one thing she could look to for comfort. And a distraction from what she might otherwise do. Lifting her sleeve, she looked at her wrist. It would be okay. It wasn't much.

Adrianna would have felt better, having seen Sean. The vision of him, buff and heroic, was enough to make any day better. A warm tingle went through her as she recalled how he looked, standing there all muscle and brawn, his warm eyes melting her. Oh, if life were different; he would have swept her up into his arms and carried her away. And there wouldn't have been a shred of resistance—not from Adrianna.

But it was a dream; she knew what Shelby had said was true. He wasn't for her. Sure, her parents would object. That was something she no longer cared about. But he seemed like a nice guy, even though her friend seemed to see him as some type of rowdy gang member. So what if he fought? Sometimes that was called for. Adrianna knew a few people that could use a tussle with someone to put them in their place. Her own father for one; at the idea of her father getting what he deserved, she nearly smiled. But not quite.

No, Sean was a good guy. That was it. Too nice for her. That was the problem. Adrianna knew what she was worthy of, and it wasn't Sean. He didn't know her well enough to be glad he'd never see her again. But if he did know, he would be glad. She wasn't his type. There was more to Adrianna than Sean could see on the surface. Much more. The thought pushed her mood toward a blackness she held fast to avoid.

She wouldn't go there. The day before, her father had upset her. Well, more than upset her. The argument had been over her propensity to sit at the computer. It annoyed him; he wanted her to work out more to stay in shape or do something constructive. Nothing she ever did was right. Recalling the crease in his forehead and the coldness of his blue eyes when he looked at her, Adrianna shuddered.

She knew better than to talk back, but Adrianna had lost it. "Leave me alone," she'd screamed. And the hard slap of her father's hand that followed had sent her flying;

her hip had banged into the dining table. The clap of his palm against her skin sounded like thunder in the small room, shocking her to reality. There was no way she'd give her father the satisfaction of seeing her cry. Fleeing to her only sanctuary, she'd locked the door behind her. There she'd reacted in the only way she knew, the only release she had.

Adrianna swore not to let it happen again. She couldn't let it. Not much longer and she'd be out of there for good, away from her parents. Adrianna hated them; despising her father more than her mother but desperate to get away from both. For the next few weeks, she'd have to avoid contact with her father, as he was easily provoked. Since he often worked late, the best plan was to eat early and go to her room, claiming lots of homework.

Her aunt was nothing like that. Even though Krista Cooper was her mother's sister, she was so much nicer. Having wealth hadn't perverted her, and she'd offered for Adrianna to come and stay with her after graduation, at least until she could afford her own place.

"It would be a pleasure," Krista had said. "After all, I'm between husbands. I would enjoy the company."

If possible, she would have left that minute but she feared her father would come after her. Graduation, the ceremony, all of it was a big deal for the Brooks. It was a chance to brag, show her off, and claim credit for their beautiful daughter. Disgusting. But Adrianna would have to suffer through it. Then she was leaving, for good.

Chapter 3

Sean leaned back on the sofa, legs splayed, lost in thought. He took another sip of the whiskey, letting it burn on the way down. Then another. And another.

He felt comfortable in his parents' home, a nice condo in a row building. His father, Patrick Reid, was a third grade teacher and well respected in the community. True, they didn't live in the expensive section of Beacon Hill; they couldn't afford it. But the home was their home and Sean was close to his family.

He relaxed on the soft fabric sofa, surrounded by the earth tones of the décor: beige walls, cream and gold rug, dark wood furniture, and dark wood floors. It was warm. It was home. He'd acquiesced when his mother asked him to stay until graduation. She'd miss him, even though the apartment he'd rented close to the business district wasn't that far away. Molli Jane Reid was a hundred percent Irish, and family was everything.

"How did the game turn out?" Bradan was Sean's younger brother by a year. They both had brown hair and were naturally muscled, which was enhanced by the hours they spent in the gym. But Sean was the tall one, whereas blue-eyed Bradan was average height, five feet eight. That didn't stop him from being a force to reckon with. Solid, sculpted muscle, and mean when someone he cared about was threatened. He was good to have around in a fight.

"It sucked. We lost."

Bradan sat across from his older brother. "What are you drinking?"

"Whiskey." Sean held the flask out. "Help yourself."

"Nah, bit early for me. What's the occasion?"

As brothers, they shared everything. Well, almost everything. And there was no confidence too private not to tell each other. That was just the way it had always been.

"Oh, a girl I met." Sean looked into space as if she might materialize right there in the living room.

"Hmm. Well, it wouldn't be the first time."

"Yes, but this girl is special. She's different."

"What's her name?"

"Adrianna Brooks. You know her?"

"Yeah, she attends private school. I've seen her picture. She won some beauty contest. Kind of a celebrity, I guess."

"How is it everybody knows her but me?"

"Well, you know her now. How'd you meet her?"

Sean recounted the story. And ended by telling Bradan that he was going to call her. "Tomas says his sister knows her. He said he'd get the number for me."

"Going after the beauty queen, huh?"

"Don't call her that."

"Didn't mean it derogatorily. She is quite something, if she looks anything in person like she does in photographs."

"She does. No picture could do justice to her beauty."

"She does sound special."

"She is, brother. She really is."

*****

Tomas came through with the phone number, and even better, the name of the school Adrianna attended. Not that great at talking on the phone, Sean decided to go to her school. Physical was better. Phones were just if you had no other alternative.

183

Tomas, Nic, and Sean piled into the Chevy, heading for the elite private school they'd only seen from the outside. Just because they couldn't attend didn't mean they couldn't visit. That was how Sean saw it. So they skipped their last class and made it to Adrianna's school before last period let out. All the way over, Sean's gut was in knots.

Having girls had never been a problem. For some reason, they were attracted to him and he often had his pick. But he never let it go to his head. They probably just liked his muscle. Something about a guy fighting excited them. Go figure.

But Adrianna was different. She wasn't just any girl. She was one of a kind. And this time he was doing the chasing, not the other way around. Sean didn't expect her to reject him, since she owed him a thank you, at least. He didn't expect her to fall into his arms either. Really, he didn't know what to expect, which was why he was all wound up about it.

The parking lot was rather empty; some students must have left early. Sean panicked for a minute, thinking he might have missed her.

"Do you see her, guys?"

"Looking," Tomas said. "That blond hair sorta stands out. Should be easy to spot."

"Keepin' my eyes peeled," Nic chimed in.

Suddenly Sean's heart began to pound. *Oh my God.* There she was, wearing a short blue skirt and ivory silk blouse. Her blond hair looked like a lion's mane, all tousled and messy, like she'd just had sex. *God.* What was he thinking?

Hesitating at the sight of her, Sean's eyes followed her long, lean legs down to the high heels that made them look a mile long.

"Do you see her? She's right there." Tomas pointed.

"Yeah, yeah, I see her, man." Before rational thought could resume, Sean pressed the accelerator and sped closer. Within a safe distance, he hit the brake and skidded the truck so it slid sideways, screeching loudly. The maneuver always impressed girls. It was so macho, the tough-guy image they liked.

But when Adrianna looked up, her eyes showed alarm at the squeal of the Chevy's tires on the blacktop. Bad start. What was he thinking? Trying to be some cool, truck-driving Irishman. Wrong approach. This was a girl used to the finer sensibilities of life—not some gang sliding toward her in an old truck.

Sean got out of the truck, afraid that she would make an escape before realizing who he was. Striding toward her, holding to a slow, steady gait so as not to alarm her further, Sean approached.

"I'm sorry. I didn't mean to scare you. Adrianna, it's Sean. Remember me?" He tried to come off relaxed, put forth a cool persona, but knowing he failed even as he attempted it.

But then she smiled. Adrianna smiled, and the whole world lit up. "Yes. Hi, Sean, I remember you."

"Didn't mean to frighten you. That's the last thing I'd want to do."

"No, you didn't. I thought it was kinda cool. How do you make it do that, skid like that?"

Sean regained confidence, boosted by her willingness to talk with him and her admiration. "Oh, it's not hard. Been doing it for years. It's just for the thrill."

"Do you often do things just for the thrill?"

That was a loaded question. "Uh, I could. I mean, maybe. Do you?"

"No, never. At this school it's unheard of." There was that beautiful smile again. Adrianna's blue eyes gleamed when she smiled. Why hadn't he remembered that? Or maybe she hadn't smiled at the ballpark. It wasn't an occasion for smiling.

"Well, you should try it sometime." Sean felt momentarily bold.

"I'd like to." The smile disappeared, almost as though Adrianna had remembered something—something important. "And anyway, I didn't thank you properly the other day. But I really appreciate you coming to the rescue. That could have ended much worse."

"Well, you're welcome. If you ever need rescuing again, I'm your guy." Sean didn't even know what he was saying. He was babbling.

"Adrianna, you ready? We gotta go." A shout came from a couple of rows over—a female voice, clearly her ride.

"It's nice to see you again, Sean. I have to go."

"Wait." Sean's heart was pounding so hard he could barely hear. She couldn't leave. If he lost her this time, it might be for good.

Adrianna stopped, her blond hair ruffling in the afternoon breeze. Her flawless skin was radiant, but the look on her face didn't reflect inner radiance to match it.

"Could I...see you? I mean, could I call you?"

Adrianna didn't move or respond. She was a perfect beauty, flawless, standing there in the middle of the parking lot looking like a blond princess.

"Sean." The way she said it didn't sound good. There was no joy. Her voice was somber, serious. What could be so bad about seeing each other? They seemed to get along okay. "Sean...I can't."

"What do you mean you can't? Why not? Do you have a boyfriend?"

"Not right now. But it wouldn't work out."

"How can you know? You don't even know me. I'm a pretty nice guy, really. If you can overlook the antics with the Chevy, I have other good qualities. I promise."

"I know you do. That's not the problem."

"What is the problem?"

"It's not something I want to talk about. I have to go. Just take my word for it, we can't see each other. We just...can't."

Adrianna didn't look any happier than Sean felt. He was crushed, and couldn't believe that she was shutting him out before they even got started. Sean watched her walk away, wanting to sweep her up and drive her off in

186

his old Chevy. So powerful was the urge that he barely resisted. He clenched his jaw and gritted his teeth. This really sucked.

When she got in the friend's car and they drove off, Sean finally went back to his truck.

"Well," Tomas said, "what happened?"

"She didn't look too happy," Nic commented.

"No, she wasn't. I don't know what happened. I really don't. She shut me out. Just like that. 'Don't call me. Thanks for the rescue. Have a good life.'"

Tomas tried to lighten the mood. "Just because the girls in our school fall all over you, doesn't mean you have universal appeal."

"Thanks for the vote of confidence, Tomas. That makes me feel a lot better."

On the way home, Sean decided that he knew the reason for her rejection. He wasn't good enough for her. Of course he wasn't. He wasn't from the right neighborhood, didn't go to the right school, didn't wear the right clothes or have the proper manners. The list was long. What could he have been thinking? That she'd fall into his arms because he saved her once?

He needed to face reality. The fact that reality wasn't *at all* what he thought it was, escaped him. Sure that he'd pegged it Sean tried to push Adrianna out of his mind. He couldn't be something he wasn't, and if that was what she needed, some high-society guy,—well, he was out of luck. He was going home. And he was getting a bottle of Irish whiskey on the way, whatever he could find. He'd need it.

Chapter 4

A year later . . .

In the dark, Adrianna gasped and bolted upright, not knowing at first where she was. Clammy skin and a feeling of fright were her first awareness. She breathed rapidly, her heart pounding, the attempt to orient in the dark creating a feeling something horrible had happened.

Then a glimpse into the present reminded Adrianna she was at her aunt's house. Her father wasn't there. She was okay; she was safe. But she didn't feel safe, only afraid. The overpowering fear settled into anxiety followed by depression. It was the same dream again.

"*No! Stop!*" Adrianna tried in vain to close off the vivid dream, but it wouldn't go away. It was like she was there all over again. Gripping the sheets, she took a few breaths. *Calm, be calm.*

The knock on her bedroom door made her jump. "Are you okay, honey?"

"Yes," she said hoarsely. "I'll be okay, Aunt Krista."

"I heard you shout."

"It was just a dream. I'm sorry I woke you."

"Okay, honey. Call if you need me."

It was the same thing, too often. The dream, waking in terror. Adrianna thought when she left home the nightmares would stop. But they didn't. They were less frequent, but just as violent. She couldn't even cry anymore.

She needed an outlet, anything. Sliding out of bed, Adrianna went to the bathroom for a drink of water. Flipping on the light, she looked at her face and didn't like what she saw: pale skin, tousled hair, and fear in her eyes. Gulping some water, she tried to release her mind from the dream still clinging to her like gloomy mist.

Closing her eyes and holding on to the edge of the marble sink, Adrianna whispered, "It's not happening now. I am okay. It's over." And then again: "It's not happening now. I am okay. It's over."

Would it ever be over? Maybe it wouldn't and she'd have to live this way forever. The torment of that idea dragged her mood down further. A frightening dream she could get over, wake up from; life, she couldn't.

Frustrated and not inclined to go back to sleep, Adrianna went to her desk and booted up the computer. A distraction, that was what she needed. Graphic design, the colors, the pixels would pull her into their vibrant scheme. Hours later, she would have new creations. Lately, it had worked.

Next to the monitor was her silver letter opener. It caught her eye, the sharp point gleaming in the muted desk lamp lighting. Her skin tingled, and she imagined it piercing into her delicate skin. For a moment she couldn't avert her eyes from it. Then suddenly, pulling from some hidden reserve of sanity, Adrianna brushed her hand across the desk, sweeping the implement off, letting it clatter to the floor.

She hugged her body and took a big breath. *I can do this.* She proceeded to log in to her programs to get to work. Deadlines were coming up. This would work out, extra time on the computer. Slowly, she became engrossed with the intricacies of design, solving those problems instead of real-life issues that refused resolution.

A few hours of work before dawn led to hours more

after the sun rose. In the nine months since graduation, Adrianna had already managed to get a couple of clients that used her regularly for their graphic needs. She was pleased; if things kept up like that, she'd be able to get her own apartment soon.

Finally, Adrianna showered and made her way to the kitchen. Alone, since her aunt was working at the gallery, she made coffee and scrambled some eggs. Her aunt didn't need to work—or so Adrianna guessed—but preferred to. As a lover of art, Krista found her work in the gallery interesting and rewarding.

That was something Adrianna understood, loving graphic art as she did, and something that annoyed her father for reasons she couldn't fathom. Actually, she was glad her aunt had left already, as she did not want to talk about the night's disruption.

Of course, her aunt suspected something was wrong, but Adrianna didn't want to discuss it. Talking about it would open the floodgates of emotion. It was difficult as it was to keep her tendencies under control. There was no chance talking to Krista would do anything but more harm.

*****

Adrianna sat on the white velvet sofa with her knees pulled up, looking down at the red patterned oriental carpet. The doorbell startled her out of reverie. Leaping up, she went to greet Kevin. Prompt as always, he'd arrived exactly at six to pick her up for dinner.

"Bye, Aunt Krista," she yelled, then opened the door and stepped outside.

Kevin stood on the porch, hands in his pockets. "Ready?" he said. His brown suede jacket hung, just so, over the blue cotton shirt that matched his eyes. Cut stylishly, his brown hair fell below the ear, spiking in just the right spots, like he'd been prepped for a photo shoot.

It occurred to Adrianna that he was exactly the type of man her parents would approve of: Protestant, rich, good looking. So why did she sometimes find him annoying?

Kevin had gone out of his way to be nice the first few months they'd dated. When Adrianna moved in with her aunt, it was a while before she'd felt like going out. But Cari, being a best friend, had urged her to socialize, and she'd met Kevin at a party.

"Yeah, ready." Adrianna forced a smile but the somber mood from the predawn hours still clung to her, despite her working all day and trying to get free of its oppression.

Kevin's jaw stiffened; his eyes glowered. At least that was what it looked like to Adrianna. "What are you wearing?"

"My new outfit, why?"

"It makes you look...too bosomy."

As if the day wasn't bad enough, he had to criticize. One thing she hated was to be criticized; she'd had too much of it all her life. Adrianna glanced down at the fitted bodice of her short dress. It was a shimmery blue color, and accented her figure. She liked it. "Well, I'm wearing it. So, are we going or not?"

Cari and her boyfriend, Samuel, were meeting them at the club. They needed to get going. Adrianna bounced down the steps and waited for Kevin. He shook his head and followed.

"You could at least wear a coat," he called after her. It was going to be that kind of evening, she guessed.

Chapter 5

Coming from the well-lit exterior to the dark interior blinded Adrianna until her eyes adjusted. She didn't know why Kevin cared what she wore anyway. With the blue, green, red, and orange strobes playing across the dance floor like colorful tubes of light, it was hard to see clothing that clearly. Colors were distorted by the rainbow beaming through the room, alternating with total darkness when the lights dimmed.

The after-hours dance club called Polarize was near many institutions of higher learning, and catered to students and the under-twenty-one crowd. No alcohol was served, which made little difference to Adrianna. She didn't drink anyway. She had her reasons.

Kevin paid the cover and guided her inside, followed by Cari and Samuel. Dancing was one of their regular weekend activities. And for Adrianna, the rock music drowned out the world. She got lost in the songs every time they went dancing, and the trendy club was one of her favorites.

Even the smell of the place—sweaty bodies, too much perfume, and cheap air freshener used to mask the first two—made Adrianna relax. Being away, lost in a crowd, hidden in the darkness, carried away by the loud music, was as close as she got to pleasure. Barely noticing Kevin, she hit the dance area and started moving.

The dress she'd worn was a good choice: light material to keep her cool, short to allow for movement, and cute so she could feel sexy. Looking through an orange light beam, Kevin's beige pants and short-sleeved shirt turned rust-colored before her very eyes. He looked better, she thought. Though handsome, he tended to dress too conservatively. A little orange did him good.

The DJ's choice of the Foo Fighters' "The Pretender" suited Adrianna. It was one she listened to a lot. Rock just didn't get better, and the group refused to be like everyone else; that was evident in their music. "Absolute genius," Cari had called the song, and it was.

When not completely absorbed in the lyrics, Adrianna took in the crowd. Dresses, fitted, short, and shimmery, and guys in pants, tight in all the right places, caught her eye. There was no dress code, so the attire ranged from attractive to raunchy with everything in between. Hairstyles were all over the chart as well: long, fluffed-out curls to short, choppy cuts. Adrianna considered doing something radical to hers, but kind of liked the long blond look.

The music slowed and Kevin put his hands on her waist, making her notice him. The lights turned dark blue, giving him a fantasy look. He smiled and started moving with the music. Adrianna moved with him, considering how nice he was to her—most of the time. He opened doors, bought flowers sometimes, was polite, and took her to good restaurants. So why didn't she feel anything? At least, not like she should have.

In the beginning, his handsomeness attracted her, and she still thought he was cute, in a preppy sort of way. Maybe things would develop. Did it always have to be love at first sight? Couldn't things build? Maybe he would grow on her. Admittedly, he had a lot of desirable qualities; likely she was too picky when she had no right to be. On that note, she decided to try and have a good time with him.

One reason Adrianna frequented that particular club was the DJ's music picks. He went from Foo Fighters to Evanescence singing "What You Want" and on to Avenged Sevenfold's "Buried Alive," a true masterpiece. Losing all track of time, Adrianna danced hard, throwing herself into the beat. She even smiled at Kevin—more than once.

Sweating and breathing hard, she nodded when Cari grabbed her elbow and pointed toward the back door. Outside was a patio where dancers could catch their breath, cool down, and get something to drink. Samuel had Cari by the hand, leading her out, and Adrianna followed with Kevin's palm on her back, guiding her.

The dim patio was missing the flood of lights they'd left, and momentarily it was a shock to the system. Spotting an empty table near the railing, Adrianna pointed. "There's a place."

Samuel wound around tables and people, leading them to the open spot. His sandy blond hair was still spiked up with gel, and when he turned to face them, Adrianna could see the sweat soaking his shirt. She could see why Cari liked him. With his green eyes, blondish hair, and lean body, he was a charmer. The fact that he had a good sense of humor, and liked to have fun, especially by dancing, gave him extra marks in the good column.

Cari looked as stick thin as ever, as annoying as that was. Adrianna had been known to starve for weeks, and never achieve the coveted emaciated look that her friend maintained with no effort. And her eyes weren't just blue; they had a gray undertone that made them exotic. It didn't hurt that Cari had big eyes, and the multiple layers of mascara slathered on her lashes gave her a fashion-model look.

"I like your dress," Adrianna said as they sat down. The shimmery gold sheath clung to Cari's slender body, finding no curves or bulges to mar the endless glitter. Adrianna had long legs, but her friend's borderline too-skinny legs seemed to go on forever.

"I just got this. It's a Natalie Baker Design."

194

"I love her stuff. We have to go shopping."

"Totally."

The server, dressed in a white stretchy top and black skirt that barely hit her upper thighs, came by and took orders. The music boomed in the main room, but was barely heard on the relatively quiet patio. Adrianna wished she were dancing again, preferring it over too much conversation. Sometimes she wondered if she had issues about interacting with others, or if she was just sick to death of it from all the events and parties her mother had dragged her to.

The cool evening felt good; as they were heated from dancing, the briskness was refreshing. Spring hadn't quite arrived, so the weather could vary from cold to warm. Even snow was a possibility that early in the year. But that night the temperatures were mild, as Boston went, and the outdoor area stayed pleasant due to patio heaters and tables of overheated dancers out to catch some air.

At least she had Cari, her best friend all through school. That made any social encounter better. Adrianna leaned toward shyness, and Cari was the opposite, outgoing and sometimes boisterous. Hanging with her took the pressure off. Conversations never lagged with Cari around.

"So, how's college?" Adrianna took a sip of her Coke.

"Uh, you know, boring mostly. I don't even know what I'm going to major in yet. My mom insisted that I go to Boston College and live at home. I don't know why I agreed; I should have gone away to college. I'm never going to get away from my parents."

Buy your copy of Perfectly Flawed today!

About The Author

Emily Jane Trent writes steamy romances about characters you'll get to know and love. The sex scenes are hot and the romance even hotter! If you are a fan of stories with a heroine that's got spunk and a hunk of a hero that you'd like to take home with you, these stories are what you're looking for. Emily's romantic tales will let you escape into a fantasy – and you won't want it to end - ever.

Dear Reader,

I hope you enjoyed this book. You are the reason I write. Feel free to communicate to me at my blog or on my fan page at Emily Jane Trent Books. Your comments are valuable. I listen. Let's chat.

Warmly,
Emily

Adam & Ella Series

This romance unfolds over four novels. Each one reveals more of the love story of Adam Bianci and Ella Walker. I hope you enjoy them!

Read them all?
Sign up for my list and you will be notified of all new releases. At www.EmilyJaneTrent.com - just click on the tab "Join Emily's List" – glad to have you.

Do you love Emily Jane Trent's romantic tales?

Let her know by telling her what you liked in a review, and leaving stars! It helps other readers make good buying decisions – they listen to you.

Made in United States
Orlando, FL
14 December 2024

55618502R10129